Praise for *Death by Chick Lit*

"A smart, fun send-up of the chick lit phenomenon—Lynn Harris's voice will reel you right in."—Elizabeth Merrick, editor of *This Is Not Chick Lit* and author of *Girly*

"Lynn Harris's clever and charming novel eviscerates the sillier corners of the New York media world while also providing a fine example of the genre she gently mocks."—Neal Pollack, author of *Alternadad*

"*Death by Chick Lit* is a wickedly funny read offering the rare combination of both teeth and heart."—Lori Gottlieb, author of *Stick Figure*

"*Death by Chick Lit* is a glamorous good time, a whodunit with some very sexy 'whos,' and a stiletto sideswipe at the sourpuss anti–chick lit movement—it's three smart/funny/cool novels in one!"—Rachel Pine, author of *The Twins of Tribeca*

"Cloning scientists should turn their attention away from sheep and focus on Lynn Harris. After reading her hilarious writing, I'm convinced the world could benefit from a dozen more comic geniuses just like her."—Andy Borowitz, author of *The Borowitz Report: The Big Book of Shockers*

"Lynn Harris's latest novel is a full-on, straight-up joy read filled with murder, mayhem, and some solutions for life's great mysteries, including our relationships with best friends, worst enemies, and the men who truly are our better halves."—Wendy Shanker, author of *The Fat Girl's Guide to Life*

DEATH BY
Chick Lit

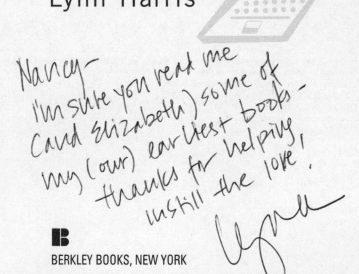

Lynn Harris

Nancy—
I'm sure you read me
(and Elizabeth) some of
my (our) earliest books—
thanks for helping
instill the love!

B
BERKLEY BOOKS, NEW YORK

THE BERKLEY PUBLISHING GROUP
Published by the Penguin Group
Penguin Group (USA) Inc.
375 Hudson Street, New York, New York 10014, USA
Penguin Group (Canada), 90 Eglinton Avenue East, Suite 700, Toronto, Ontario M4P 2Y3, Canada
(a division of Pearson Penguin Canada Inc.)
Penguin Books Ltd., 80 Strand, London WC2R 0RL, England
Penguin Group Ireland, 25 St. Stephen's Green, Dublin 2, Ireland (a division of Penguin Books Ltd.)
Penguin Group (Australia), 250 Camberwell Road, Camberwell, Victoria 3124, Australia
(a division of Pearson Australia Group Pty. Ltd.)
Penguin Books India Pvt. Ltd., 11 Community Centre, Panchsheel Park, New Delhi—110 017, India
Penguin Group (NZ), 67 Apollo Drive, Rosedale, North Shore 0745, Auckland, New Zealand
(a division of Pearson New Zealand Ltd.)
Penguin Books (South Africa) (Pty.) Ltd., 24 Sturdee Avenue, Rosebank, Johannesburg 2196,
South Africa

Penguin Books Ltd., Registered Offices: 80 Strand, London WC2R 0RL, England

This book is an original publication of The Berkley Publishing Group.

This is a work of fiction. Names, characters, places, and incidents either are the product of the author's imagination or are used fictitiously, and any resemblance to actual persons, living or dead, business establishments, events, or locales is entirely coincidental. The publisher does not have any control over and does not assume any responsibility for author or third-party websites or their content.

PRINTING HISTORY
Berkley trade paperback edition / June 2007

Library of Congress Cataloging-in-Publication Data

Harris, Lynn.
    Death by chick lit / Lynn Harris.—Berkley trade pbk. ed.
        p.   cm.
    ISBN 978-0-425-21524-1 (pbk.)
    1. Women novelists—Fiction.   2. Murder—Investigation—Fiction.   3. Brooklyn (New York, N.Y.)—
Fiction.   4. Chick lit.   I. Title.

PS3608.A78325D43   2007
813'. 6—dc22

                                                                                2006102097

PRINTED IN THE UNITED STATES OF AMERICA

10   9   8   7   6   5   4   3   2   1

For David and Bess

ACKNOWLEDGMENTS

My profound thanks to Paula Balzer, Kate Seaver, Chris Kalb, Colin Lingle, Betsy Fast, Juliet Eastland, Marjorie Ingall, Wendy Shanker, Carolyn Mackler, Judy Bornstein, Amy Keyishian, Jason Jacobs, Jim Gaylord, Michael Lee, Dixie Feldman, Jim and Florence Harris, Saul and Betty Adelson, Anna Adelson, and, of course, David Adelson, for their invaluable contributions to this book, and to my life.

Death by Chick Lit

One

Where on earth was Mimi McKee?

How could she miss her own book party?

Lola Somerville sipped her Mimi-tini and tried not to think evil thoughts.

Well, she tried.

Mimi had not even been a *writer* writer until now. Before, she'd just been a plucky publicist whose letter to the editor defending the "gay best friend" as a real person, not just a stock character, had scored her a book deal practically overnight. Hence her novel, *Gay Best Friend*, and the accompanying movie option by Cameron Diaz's production company. Plus this super-schmancy publication party at Cabin 9—with a drink named after the author, no less.

I will not be petulant, Lola thought. I like Mimi. I have my health. I have wonderful friends. I have a loving husband, and I mean that in a true-life-partner way, not in a "Husband: *check*!" way. I am happy. So, what? I don't deserve a supercool book party with free Somerville Slings?

Whoops. Lola caught herself. Positive: 0, Petulant: 1.

Okay, she conceded, I'm just going to think these thoughts once, and then they will be out of my system.

Everyone gets better book parties than mine. Everyone gets better book deals than mine. Everyone's book gets better buzz than mine. Everyone's book is ranked higher on Amazon than mine, even when everyone else's reviews all have only one star. Everyone has an "idea for a book"—or one landing in their lap. Can someone maybe throw me a bone here? How about a call from an editor saying she wants to hear more of my voice? An e-mail from a fancy agent saying, "I've seen your work and I've got the perfect book idea for you! See six-figure contract, attached."

Just once, Lola whimpered to herself, can't I write some random article and have Jodie Foster phone me, out of the blue, ready to make it into a film? Or jeez, okay, Minnie Driver. Just *something*.

Lola scowled in the dim light, then held her hand up. Okay, she thought. Done. I've met my crappy karma quota for the night.

She hoisted her rotini-twisty red hair—which she'd hated as a kid but now realized was her best asset—into a plastic clip, ten to a pack, from Duane Reade. As Lola frequently observed, she'd be a dead ringer for Nicole Kidman if she were two feet taller and had a different face. Hers, nose included, was rounder and flecked with freckles, though in random positions from her forehead to her chin, not the official "cute" constellation of nose and upper cheeks. But her smile was wide and easy, and her shining green eyes reminded her husband, he often said, of the best olives he'd ever eaten, back on some crazy adventure in Crete with a loaded former roommate. "Whenever I look at you, I think of salt and sun," he liked to say. "Is there any way you could spend less time blinking?"

Lola scanned the room's dark log walls. Party guests jammed the bar three deep and reclined here and there on vintage metal bunk beds. Tree-tall waitresses, all midriff, passed Hi-C shots and trays of s'mores. Lola squinted at people's faces, hard-pressed to make them out. What was that Fox News special report on how women's health declines more rapidly if they haven't had at least one baby by age twenty-two? Didn't they say night vision was one of the first things to go?

Ah! A clue! Somewhere in the swirl, Lola spotted Mimi's newish boyfriend, Quentin, a good egg if there ever was one, though on the breakable side. Alas, Mimi was not at his side. Quentin excused himself from a clot of well-wishers and headed for a door.

Huh. Guess he's looking for her, too. Lola knew from her experience with Mimi in book club, which was where they'd met, and which Lola had quit when the group had voted nine to one to reread *The Bridges of Madison County* on the anniversary of its publication, that Mimi was always twenty minutes early to everything. So where on earth is she? And speaking of missing people, where is Annabel? She totally swore she was coming to give me moral support. And where, for that matter, is my husband, who will take me away from all this and score me a second goody bag?

Lola found an empty spot on a picnic table bench and crossed one painted wooden clog over the other, a little bummed, on top of everything, that she hadn't worn her favorite cowboy boots on what was likely to be her last cool evening out before the mid-June boot solstice. She yanked her Loehmann's Black Dress—LBD, as she and Annabel called them—down over her knees and reviewed the evening so far. Her plan had been simply this: congratulate Mimi sincerely, torment herself briefly, and then go out with her husband and her best friend for a bite to eat, if there indeed remained any restaurant nearby that served anything but "small plates." Okay, Lola thought, one out of three.

She polished off her Mimi-tini, golden-retrievering her tongue into the glass to make sure she hadn't missed anything.

Hmm. Who's that coming toward me? Lola wondered. As far as she could make out, the figure, head tilted toward a cell phone on her shoulder, was not the object of her guilty umbrage, nor of her recent wedding vows. Hell's bells, Lola thought. Whoever this is, I am disinclined to make small talk about how my book is going, because it's not.

"Mimi, it's me! Where the eff are you?!? Call me the second you get this!" Even over the music, Lola recognized the voice speaking into the phone before the low-ponytailed woman fully emerged from the shadows, clipping along in shoes with toes so pointy they must have just been sharpened. It was Mimi's approximately eleven-year-old book publicist, Holly Something. Holly, in fact, had been Lola's book publicist for ten minutes before getting promoted. Spotting Lola, Holly said, "Oh hi, Kim!" and punched up another number on her spangled Sidekick.

Change of scenery—*now*, thought Lola. She headed for the restroom, wondering vaguely if the party would merit an appearance by the total It Girl Crystal sisters, the hard-partying, cross-dressing heirs to a vast aspartame fortune. She passed knots of Mimi's friends, professional publishing party attendees, and, notably, Blanca Palette, who was entitled to feel even surlier than Lola. Blanca's eyes were perpetually downcast—you could just hear an aunt saying, "You'd be so pretty if you'd look up and *smile!*"— and her ears stuck out from her wispy brown hair ("Have you considered getting a permanent?"). Blanca wrote Serious Books with female protagonists that consistently received reviews along the lines of "Chick lit with brains!" and then sold fewer copies than their lighter counterparts.

Lola felt Blanca's pain. She had nothing against chick lit itself, or its authors, Mimi included. To her, the catch-all, now-derisive term and the snooty, apocalyptic attitude toward the genre was the problem. Ever since Bridget Jones—whom Lola considered a classic screwball heroine, not some sort of tipsy antipioneer—it seemed that every book written by a woman or with a female protagonist was now labeled *chick lit.* (While anything written by a guy was, of course, *lit.*) According to assorted stern reviewers and opinion writers, chick lit—which, like any genre, had its more or less distinguished iterations—was itself responsible for the decline of Western literature. It was, at the very least, "bad for women," a charge—as Lola herself had written in many letters to the editor that had never been optioned—that implied, condescendingly, that women can't tell the difference between instruction manuals and entertainment. Some journalists had already declared the genre "dead," but obviously, editors were still buying, and nothing had stopped that one curmudgeon at the *New Yorker* from calling the newest edition of *The Guns of August* "military chick lit."

The whole matter had hit especially close to home lately for Lola. As a freelance magazine writer and former online advice columnist—who, up until the dot-com bust, had had a pretty serious following—she'd done pretty well for herself. She'd been writing professionally in one form or another since college, where she'd been a bit of a big journo on campus; after that, she'd jumped right into local reporting, eventually breaking into national glossies and their crunchier, more political counterparts. Then came AskLola.com, and then Lola's ill-fated tenure at the now-extinct women's media giant, Ovum, Inc.

Lola's novel, *Pink Slip*, was her account—fictionalized into a mystery/thriller/whodunit—of her own successful investigation into Ovum's villainous wrongdoing and spectacular demise. Her publisher had duly positioned *Pink Slip* as a "seriously hard-hitting *and* entertainingly readable exposé: in the truth-through-fiction tradition of Christopher Buckley, a story about the story behind the biggest media scam of our era." The press, in turn, had labeled it "the hilarious misadventures of America's newest titian-haired sleuth."

If this chick lit classification had been accurate—or, frankly, a sales-booster—that would have been fine, Lola had figured. Instead, *Pink Slip* had gotten neither the pop-commercial success that should have come with the chick lit label nor the writer's writer accolades that should have come without it. Her agent was ready for her to "try again," but Lola, who was really proud of *Pink Slip*, wasn't quite ready to let go.

Also, she was out of new ideas.

This she knew, at least: no *pink* in the title. Not even if it was about Communism.

As Lola excuse-me'd her way through the crowd on her way downstairs, bonking into people with the giant shoulder bag that held everything she needed for the day, for the next thirty days, she reflected on the personal progress she'd made over the past few years. She used to call Annabel from the ladies' room to report on dates. Now she'd call Annabel from the ladies' room to report on her career. So that was a step. Unfortunately, the news in the career department was, these days, almost always nonexistent.

Marriage doesn't fix your life, thought Lola. This she had learned.

Lola started to push open the restroom door. No checking voice mail, she resolved; just a quick call to Annabel to make sure she was on her damn way. If Mimi was going to make some sort of grand late entrance, she wanted to be there to silently resent it.

Except this wasn't the restroom.

The cool nightclubs had no sign outside; the *really* cool nightclubs had no sign outside or on the bathroom doors. Having attended her share of book parties, this wasn't the first time Lola had walked into a supply closet.

But this was the first time she had sensed something very, very wrong.

I did not just see a foot, Lola thought, opening the door wider to make sure. A chunk of gray light fell in from the hall.

Oh, *there's* Mimi.

Covered in blood.

The broken martini glass that had slit her throat lay nearby.

In the 0.03 of a second before she screamed and passed out, Lola felt really, really guilty.

TWO

Lola blinked. All she could see was television snow. She blinked again. Her arm ached where she must have smacked the doorframe on her way down; her filmy poncho hadn't served as much cushion. But the snow was starting to clear, and from her one other experience with fainting—which was the one time she'd tried acupuncture, which she did only because someone said it would help her get a new literary agent, so really, she deserved to have passed out—she knew just what to expect this time. She would blink once again, and then open her eyes to see, clustered above her, a hazy circle of concerned faces: her mother, her husband, Doug, I'kea the bodyworker, Bella, Abzug, and Steve, her Weimaraner mix from childhood. And then everything would be all right. And I'kea, kind soul, wouldn't even charge her.

Lola went for it. She opened her eyes once more. Ah, there was the cluster of heads.

But hey! They weren't even looking at her.

Figures, thought Lola, sinking her head back down.

Oh, wait.

She turned her head. That stale, musty smell was not dog

breath. The guy in the jacket and tie? Can't be Abzug: no hat. And the one with rubber gloves? Most certainly not Doug. And— as Lola now finally, clearly, gut-flippingly recalled—someone had performed an altogether less healthy type of bodywork on Mimi McKee.

Lola sat up on her good elbow.

Don't look don't look don't look—*uch*, you looked.

A gloved EMT was just pulling a sheet over Mimi's face.

I really, really, need to not be where that body is, Lola thought. Oh, Mimi's poor mom.

As Lola bent a knee and put one clog on the floor to stand up, the jacket and tie guy—must be a detective—noticed that she'd come to.

"Welcome back," he said, not smiling. At least he was blocking the view of Mimi. It occurred to Lola that his dimensions might actually be square. His black hair was slicked back, perpendicular to his mustache, and he had those thick oversized glasses that make the wearer look a bit like a grouper. Which reminded Lola of someone.

"Detective Bobbsey," he said. "You all right?"

"Relatively," Lola said. She grabbed his outstretched hand and hauled herself onto her feet. "Thanks. Bobbsey?" Lola asked before she could stop to think. "Is your partner your twin?" She immediately regretted her impertinence, though she had nothing but respect for the Bobbsey Twins mysteries of her youth.

"Nope," he said. "My partner is my wife. Maternity leave. Due in a couple weeks. They still haven't found me my requisite rookie replacement." His arm behind Lola's shoulders, he guided her out into the hall. She didn't look back.

"Well, congratulations," Lola said. "Your first child?" Was that what you were supposed to ask? she wondered.

"Thanks, and yes, our first," he answered, then deadpanned, ". . . that we know of . . ." in air quotes. He looked about ten years older than her, maybe; seemed to Lola like he'd have a whole brood of squarish children by now. "And thanks for the straight line," Bobbsey added, still not smiling. "Mind answering a few questions?" He raised a teeny memo pad and poised his golf pencil. Why do detectives always have unsatisfactory note-taking equipment, Lola wondered. Maybe his partner-to-be will be green enough to bring a couple of decent Papermates to the relationship.

"No problem at all," said Lola. She felt a sudden wicked thrill, the thrill of being in on something, close to something. Then, just as quickly, she felt like an ass. Hi, Lola? Mimi is dead. *That* is what you're in on, she thought. I know I have to talk to Bobbsey, but boy, do I need to see Doug's face.

"You a friend of hers?" asked Bobbsey, nodding back toward the storeroom of death.

"Not close, but I know her. Knew her," said Lola.

"I'm sorry," said Bobbsey, adjusting his glasses. "What were you doing down here?" he asked.

"Going to the bathroom," Lola said. "I mean, looking for it."

Bobbsey nodded. "Did you see anyone else around?"

"No, I didn't."

Hell's bells. Does this mean I don't have an alibi? Do I have to call a lawyer? Who do I know? Lola racked her brain. C'mon, I must know one attorney who doesn't do environmental law or electronic civil liberties. "You don't think I—"

"Slit her throat, wiped the blood off your hands, and then fainted?" asked Bobbsey.

Right. "Not so much," said Lola. You go, Miss Marple.

"Detective, buddy, you got a sec?" Apparently someone had talked his way past whoever was guarding the stairs. Someone tall-ish and thinnish, with reddish wavy hair and freckles he could stand to outgrow. Someone who looked incredibly familiar.

"Nope," said Bobbsey.

"Okay, how about now?" asked the interloper.

"Nope."

Oh, for God's sake, thought Lola. It had come to her.

I totally went on a date with that guy.

Lola's mother's friend Fern—this fellow's aunt—had set them up forty-eleven years ago. ("You're both single, you're both writers, and you both have red hair and freckles!" she'd exclaimed.) The two of them had had a perfectly nice time, which was the kind of date Lola used to hate the most. If you don't have a great time, you at least deserve a good story.

Neither he nor Lola had seemed to have any interest in a second perfectly nice time, and that had been that. Lola had not thought about Wally at all on the way home—this had been her litmus test for whether or not to see someone again—and therefore not at all thereafter. He had left her a voice mail just to say thanks, but that was it. He was not even looking at her right now.

"Wally Seaport, *New York Day*." He extended a hand to the detective.

Sure enough. Wally was a reporter for the tabloid *New York Day*, whose weekly chick lit bestseller list had once been a weekly source of torment for Lola. Everyone knew Wally also wrote *Royalty*, the must-read blog for the New York publishing industry. *Royalty* was impossible to describe without using the word *snarky*, but given its success and taste-making status, the *Day* looked the other way, even though Wally's posts openly mocked its shameless tabloid style. They requested of Wally only that, for the sake of appearances, he use an open-secret pseudonym. Lola had quit reading both the blog and the *Day* when her yoga teacher had said something about "being compassionate enough with yourself to limit the 'shoulds' that serve only to cause stress." Which for Lola also included yoga, but whatever.

Lola also knew for a fact—though she thought she'd gotten over it—that *Royalty* had never once mentioned *Pink Slip*. (Her yoga teacher had never said anything about limiting the Googling.) Wally had to have known about the book. Not only had she gotten a pretty decent advance—the kind of thing Wally normally snooped out and reported in his weekly "Lucky Them" list—but *Pink Slip* was itself about a media scandal. If that wasn't *Royalty* material, Lola didn't know what was. Why the snub? Right now, standing not twenty feet from the murdered body of someone she considered a friend, Lola was ashamed to feel the sting of wounded pride start to flare anew.

"Hi," Lola said to Wally, as nicely as possible.

"Evening." Wally nodded, still not looking. "Now?" he asked Bobbsey.

Jeez Louise. He doesn't remember me a bit. Not even a glimmer.

"Maybe, maybe when I'm done talking to this young lady," Bobbsey replied. "Can you give us a minute?"

Wally hesitated.

The detective didn't. "How about now?" Bobbsey asked.

Wally backed off and pretended to be very absorbed in his notes.

"So. Sorry, miss. How well did you know Miss McKee?" Bobbsey asked. Lola knew Wally was listening. Maybe she could drop a hint that would trip some sort of memory wire.

"We're—we were—friendly acquaintances, I guess," said Lola. "I mean, we're both, you know, *writers*—"

"She have a boyfriend?"

"Yes, she does. Did."

Oh my God, poor Quentin.

"Oh, really?" asked Bobbsey.

"Yes," said Lola. Quentin and Mimi hadn't been dating for long—maybe two months?—but as far as Lola could tell, it had appeared to be heading toward the magic three.

"Really?!" asked Bobbsey again. "Like, steady?"

"Uh, yes, steady," said Lola, puzzled. "You sound surprised."

"I mean . . . well, I mean, the book," said Bobbsey.

"The book . . ."

"The book. Miss McKee's book. I thought you had to be, like, perpetually single and unhappy to write that stuff, the chick flicks or whatever you call them," said Bobbsey. "I mean, I don't know, it seemed really, you know, true-to-life to me."

Lola had to smile. Wally shot the detective a look. "It was in my wife's beach bag." Bobbsey shrugged. "I thought it was great. Really funny." He glanced back toward the storeroom. "Poor kid."

I love this guy, thought Lola. "Yeah. Chick lit. They're not necessarily a hundred percent autobiographical," she said. Sensing an opportunity, she went on a bit too loud. "I mean, *even my recent book*, while based on fact, was mostly fictionalized."

Wally didn't bat an eye.

Damn.

Bobbsey nodded, all business once again. "So, the boyfriend," he prompted.

"Right," said Lola. "Poor guy." Lola opted not to mention that she'd dated Quentin, too. Very, very briefly. Years ago. Not pertinent.

"He got a name?"

"Quentin. Quentin Frye." The detective scribbled in his notebook. Quentin can be more help than I can, Lola figured. He might know if Mimi had some sort of cyberstalker, had received any threats, that kind of thing.

"Thank you very much, Miss—"

"Ms.," really, but anyway. "*Lola Somerville*." Zero reaction from Wally. Unreal.

She gave Bobbsey her number. He offered a card in return. "Call us if you remember anything else. Why don't we all go upstairs now." It was not a question.

"Excuse me—" said Wally.

"You, too, c'mon up. We'll give you something outside." They were already halfway down the hall. It was too late for Wally to argue.

"Time to talk to the boyfriend," Bobbsey said to the empty

space ahead of him. Then he looked back at Lola, a flicker of sorrow behind his big square lenses. "It's always the boyfriend."

No way, thought Lola. No *way*. It can't be. He can't be. *Cannot* be. And not just because I was the one who set Quentin and Mimi up.

Three

Quentin wouldn't hurt a mouse, this Lola knew for sure. He would attempt to *avoid* hurting a mouse by setting a glue trap, but he would also forget that he'd eventually have to find a way to *dispose* of sticky Mickey. Lola had learned this the first and last time she'd slept at Quentin's place. They'd just *slept* slept, for the record—which, you see, is what happens sooner than you mean it to when you live in Brooklyn and your suitor lives on the Upper East Side of Manhattan. Because while Brooklyn and Manhattan indeed share a mayor and are separated only by one narrow river, as far as cabdrivers and Manhattan dwellers are concerned—who, by the way, think it's never-fail hilarious to ask if they need a passport to cross the bridge—the distance between the two boroughs might as well be, oh, 508 miles, which is the mathematical difference between Brooklyn's underdog 718 area code and Manhattan's coveted 212.

That morning, when Lola had been trying to clear out of Quentin's apartment as quickly as possible, a yelp had brought her jogging into the kitchen, with only one contact lens in so far.

"What? Are you okay?" Lola squinted. She could barely make out the form of Quentin, handsome, scary-smart, well-meaning Quentin, Quentin with a bit of an old soul, Quentin who favored comfortable suede English teacher shoes and who accepted though didn't quite understand Lola's good-natured ribbing about how he'd worn a sweater vest on their first date, Quentin who wrote crossword puzzles for a syndication service and owned his own once-used rice cooker, Quentin who was losing a bit of his fine blond hair, but only from a bird's-eye view, Quentin who was sitting on a kitchen stool, gripping its sides, staring at an open door beneath his sink.

"Quentin, what the dilly?"

"Lola? Can you do me a favor?" His voice was steady, but only with effort.

"Does it require binocular vision?" she asked.

"Can you get rid of the mouse under the sink?"

Lola winked her useless left eye closed, grabbed a piece of paper towel, picked up the poor creature—who, the trap's "humane" intentions notwithstanding, had succumbed—dropped it into the blue plastic bag in which the *New York Times* had arrived, took out the trash, washed her hands, put in her left contact, found Quentin in the kitchen, and said, "You know what? I'm not sure this is going to work out."

Quentin and Lola were indeed cut out to be friends, nothing more. She didn't mind getting rid of the mouse; she just needed to be with someone who, you know, *could* get rid of a mouse. And now, friends was definitely all they were, their brief past the most non of nonissues. She'd still e-mail Quentin now and then to find a five-letter word for *Caspian tributary*, or at least a hint on the name of the second musketeer. He'd playfully refuse, and they'd e-mail back and forth nonetheless, trying to "coordinate" to get together, finally trailing off and falling back out of touch, until Lola needed an eleven-letter word for *expedient*.

Quentin was really not cut out to be a killer.

I'm sure the cops will figure that out on their own, Lola thought. I'd rather not embarrass him by telling them about the mouse.

She and Bobbsey, Wally trailing, made it back upstairs into the club, now brightly lit and nearly empty but for a couple of somber waitresses collecting their purses. Lola looked around. With a flick of the light switch, Cabin 9 had gone from dim and sleek to garish and clunky. The picnic benches looked beat-up and splintery, creating a heretofore unseen hazard to panty hose. The bunk beds, once funkily enticing, looked dingy and depressing. And the *mattresses!* Eew. You know what hides dirt? Lola thought. *Darkness.*

The sidewalk in front of the club was still clotted with partygoers, every one of whom was talking on a cell phone. The spinning yellow lights of three parked cop cars tiddlywinked off the slick, just-rained-on street. A cluster of women dressed in black, soggy signs leaning against their shins, lingered half a block up the Bowery. One was talking to a cop.

Oh, them.

The Jane Austen Liberation Front. The JALF could be counted on to protest every single chick lit reading or party, insisting that the genre cheapened both literature and women. Their leader, Wilma Vouch, who'd chained herself to Barnes & Noble the day *Bridget Jones* hit American stores, was not someone you'd want on your bad side. So, as far as the low JALF turnout at her own book party was concerned, Lola had never complained.

Lola looked back around the crowd. "I don't see Quentin," she said to Bobbsey. Good.

"It's okay, we'll get ahold of him."

"Lola!"

Finally.

It was Lola's newly minted husband, Doug, her best friend, Annabel, and Annabel's friend Leo, whom Lola was secretly much happier to see than any of Annabel's various other consorts. Leo served as Annabel's gentleman walker to most parties, as she openly admitted that most of her suitors didn't "get along that well with humans."

"Are you okay?" Doug kissed Lola just to the left of her still-bright lipstick.

"Yeah, I think so," said Lola. It was really, really good to see him. "I found the body, you know."

"What?!"

"Hang on." She gestured at Bobbsey. "Well, here's my card," she said, feeling silly, as she'd already given him her number—but this particular card bore the title of her book. Who knew? Maybe *Pink Slip* would wind up in his wife's beach bag.

"Lola, seriously." Lola had turned back to face her friends, arms dangling limp at her sides. Annabel, concern showing in her nearly violet eyes, took hold of Lola's elbows. "*Are* you okay?"

Lola looked at her. It was really, really good to see Annabel, too. What was that study she'd read about? The one where husbands said their wives were their best friends, but wives said their best friends were their best friends?

"I mean, Lo, you look worse than that night we . . . did that thing Doug doesn't know about," Annabel said, a sly smile curving her lips to the left. Lola couldn't help but laugh. Doug, accustomed to being double-teamed, smiled and shook his head. Leo, Lola noticed, looked fleetingly peeved.

"No no, yeah, I'm fine," said Lola. She took a breath and started to tell the whole story. By the time she got to the Wally Seaport part, though, she was really flagging. The survival dose of adrenaline served up by her hippocampus was dissipating, and she was starting to feel foggy and twitchy. Distracted, she watched two of the cop cars pull away.

"Holy moly, Lola," said Leo, filling the silence. He looked cute in his white shirt and jeans, the outfit Lola was always trying to get Doug to wear. It made Lola forgive Leo the goatee. "What an experience. I bet you could use a drink."

"Oh, no thanks, Leo, I'm good."

"No thanks? *You?* Wait, are you pregnant?"

Doug blushed.

"Leo, I just *fainted.*"

"Oh yeah. Sorry." He reddened. Annabel's purple-streaked braids swung as she fished a bottle of Poland Springs out of her threadbare knapsack and handed it to Lola.

"I know your contract says Evian, but it's the best I can do," said Annabel. She had a wee silver stud in her nose, rings on thumbs and toes, and a tiny black-and-white tattoo of Bettie Page's head on her hip. Bettie's famous black bangs, matching Annabel's, were visible just above the waistband of her low-slung fatigues.

"Thanks," said Lola. She gulped down the entire bottle while her friends watched. Except Leo, who was watching Annabel. Even amid other distractions, the ladies, they notice such things.

"Where were you guys, anyway?" asked Lola.

"Subway hell," said Doug, taking off his clunky glasses—Lola loved it when he skipped his contacts—and rubbing his army-green eyes. "Report of a suspicious package at Bleecker Street. Turned out Mayor Bloomberg had left his briefcase on the train."

"But they shut down *everything,* so these guys were trapped downtown, and I was stuck coming from uptown," added Leo.

"Anyway, this is totally insane and gross and terrifying," said Annabel, sticking her hands in the pockets of her worn hoodie. No makeup, as usual. Upper East Side women always stopped Annabel at her schmancy gym—a single date with the owner had yielded Annabel a lifetime membership—to ask her where she got her eyelashes perma-dyed. She didn't, of course; they were just that long and dark. "Who would have anything against Mimi?" Annabel asked. "I mean, besides you?"

"Hey. I wanted to kill her, but I didn't want to *kill* her," said Lola. "And don't forget, it could have been just a stranger, some random crazy person, I don't know."

Right then, a reflection caught her eye, along with a familiar face behind it. She turned. The light had caught a pair of big square glasses, like Detective Bobbsey's, only they were not on Bobbsey's face. And this grouper, this guy lurking twenty yards away near a scaffold, Lola recognized: it was Reading Guy.

Reading Guy! Reading Guy came to pretty much every single chick lit reading, ever. Everyone knew who he was. He'd been sighted at the downtown Borders, the uptown Y, and everywhere in between. Fortyish and pasty, he wore suspenders on brown acrylic pants, his top shirt button buttoned, the bottom two not, and ancient black sneakers with black laces. His glasses were so large that the bottom edges rested on his cheeks. Every book reading, he'd come and sit in the back, listen intently, and lurk, sweating slightly even in winter. He never bought a book or had one signed, but there he'd stand, next to a shelf, upright and silent, until the last guest left. Reading Guy never crossed a line, but everyone wished he would so they could actually ask him to leave. You know, so he could go home and work on his "wallpaper"— Scotch-taped collages of creased chick lit covers and yellowed reviews and grimy authors' photos marked with runic grease pencil. At least that's what everyone imagined.

In short, Reading Guy freaked people out.

Including Lola, at that very moment. She'd never heard of a Reading Guy sighting anywhere but a bookstore, yet there he was right now, right there, looking particularly lurky.

I should tell the cops.

"Hang on, guys," Lola said, turning quickly to look for Bobbsey. She heard a car door slam a short way back up the block. It was one of those unmarked cop sedans. Lola could make out Bobbsey in the passenger seat. The car revved and began to move away.

"Hey!" Lola called. "Hey!" Her hippocampus was firing hard again, and Lola was suddenly zinging with energy like a cartoon guy with his finger in a socket. "There's something I should tell you!" Now she was jogging. "It's Reading Guy! Reading Guy is here!" Just as she reached the back door of the car, it pulled onto the Bowery and sped away. All she saw was Quentin, sitting in the backseat.

Lola turned back toward her friends, only to see Reading Guy start to run the other way.

Four

"C'mon you guys, let's go after him!" Lola wheeled on her heel and started sprinting back the way Reading Guy had run.

Did I just say, "Let's go after him?"

The moment Lola reached her posse, they reached out and snared her like a bug in a web.

"Come on!" she protested, struggling. "It was Reading Guy!"

"Lola, are you high?" asked Annabel.

"A little," she said, wiggling only weakly now. *Yeah,* she thought grimly. *High on death.*

"Reading Guy is beyond creepy," said Annabel, who knew all about him from Lola. "But that doesn't mean he killed Mimi, or that you can run in clogs."

"Didn't the detective give you his number?" asked Leo, ever helpful. "Why don't you just call him right now with a description?"

At this point Lola had collapsed onto Doug, who was stroking her hair, or at least trying to organize it. She nodded and reached for her cell. The emergency coping hormones were fading for good, and so was she. It had been a long, vile night.

"And then let's go home," Doug said.

Lola and Doug lived farther out in Brooklyn than most Manhattanites would venture, even under terrorist threat. While the nearby up-and-came areas had charming brownstones, *really* famous authors, and beatific twins wearing CBGB's onesies, Lola and Doug's apartment was in a kind of no-man's-land marked by vacant lots and vinyl siding. It hadn't had a name until area Realtors, agents of gentrification doom, had invented one to make it sound more like the nicer neighborhood a short distance south, which was called Wayside. So now Lola and Doug's neighborhood was called, at least in the real estate classifieds, North Wayside. Sounded inviting, but few were willing to make the trek, even for Doug's cooking. Their Manhattan friends called it NoWay.

Still, Lola had realized her lifelong dream of having a garden and living near water. The water, it should be noted, was the diner-coffee-colored Lundy Canal, lined by the backs of warehouses and dotted here and there by the motorboats of the brave. Doug called it Rio Stinko. The canal, you see, had been used for centuries as a repository for waste both chemical and human, including bullet-riddled bodies. Urban legend told that the water was so polluted, it had once caught fire. But developers' leering eyes had, of course, spotted the canal, which meant, first, good things for the environment (clean water) and, then, less good (the inevitable Cleanwater Canalside Café). A flushing and revitalization project was indeed under way, already touting great strides in water clarity and renewed populations of dinoflagellates, which, Lola imagined, was the scientific name for "big fish who smack themselves for living there." Even they, one day, would likely be priced out.

Lola's garden was, like tiny blue crabs in the canal, another minor urban miracle. Their apartment was a converted— barely—"industrial space," and industrial spaces don't have backyards. So Lola's green thumb—inherited from and nurtured by her father—had pointed out front. Certainly no one had ever planted anything there before in the nearly bare dirt between the front of the building and the sidewalk; when they'd moved in, the only vegetation was cigarette butts, Jolly Rancher wrappers, and the long, tapered, half-buried leg of a Barbie, which Doug had uprooted before it grew any taller.

But Lola had rolled up her sleeves and gone to work, taking cabs home from garden stores and ordering eco-friendly squirrel repellent online. And now, when you walked the ten minutes to Lola and Doug's place from the nearest subway, past the casket company whose doors, offering dubious welcome, were always open, past the one bodega with the sun-faded cans of motor oil and Pringles in the window, past the funny new store that sold only doorknobs—which always made Lola feel bad for not being a regular, but then again, really, how much doorknob turnover do you have?—then, just as you spotted the creaky metal bridge over Rio Stinko in the near distance and wondered why the heck you ever left Manhattan, you'd see it.

Is that a sunflower?

Actually, that would be five sunflowers. At the height of the season, that would also be morning glories, nasturtiums, honeysuckle, jasmine, and five kinds of basil. Plus hollyhocks, foxglove, lilies, lupine. Portulaca, clematis, lavender. Any herb you'd ever want in an omelet. Hot chili peppers, too. And tomatoes. Ignoring all instructions to "plant seedlings twenty-four inches apart," Lola had filled two roughly seven-by-seven rectangles on either side of the front steps—plus two other small stretches between the sidewalk and the street—with tall, jungly tangles of all the sun-loving plants she'd never been able to grow indoors, even with enough Gro-Lites to make her apartment look like it was set up for a photo shoot (specifically, a photo shoot of ailing plants). She had suffered for years with just a couple of coleuses, the requisite bathroom fern, and one desultory philodendron with whom she was never quite on speaking terms, waiting all the while for a knight in shining armor to carry her off into the full sun.

And in rode her geek-hottie hybrid dreamboat Doug, who would have done so on a Segway if he hadn't instead been saving for a down payment with someone like Lola. Doug of the thick, dark hair Lola loved to put a hand in and just hold, Doug who could build a computer out of a coconut and a website out of thin air, Doug who was still in touch with his friends from his D&D days, Doug who could sort of play the banjo. Their love was the phoenix that had risen, two years before, and faster than anyone had expected, from the ashes of their dot-com glory days at Ovum, Inc.

So Lola had Doug, and because of Doug, she had her garden. It was her pride, her joy, her most beloved procrastination. Having returned to freelance journalism, Lola worked at home. Whenever she got sick of no one calling about her novel, she'd step out and deadhead the marigolds.

The night of Mimi's murder, Doug bundled Lola into a cab—a $30 splurge for them, plus a twenty-five minute ride with a glowering driver sure he'd never pick up a fare for the way back—and stroked her hair with her head on his lap, which was her second-favoritest thing ever in the whole wide world, but she was too spent at that moment to reposition for him to scratch her back.

"See?" said Lola drowsily. "If we had kids, or even a dog, we'd never be able to go out on the town like this."

"And find dead bodies?" asked Doug.

"Well, you know."

Oh, how she loved him. How did she know? Because she loved hanging out with him. They always had a good time. They *liked* each other. They were fine apart, of course—they'd always drift away from each other at parties to allow each other more airtime—but their druthers were to be together. So many people forget that, Lola thought. That in addition to any lightning-strike love, there also has to be *like*. You actually have to *like* each other, *want* to be together, feel like you *need* to be in the same place at the same time, even if one of you is lost in a book and the other is scrambling an egg.

Now that she and Doug were married, though, something had shifted a bit—not in Lola's devotion, but in her intentions. Lola was highly determined not to become one of those married women who, due to their "lifestyle change," stop seeing their single friends. She hung out constantly with Annabel, dutifully did the requisite girl brunches, made sure she went to media parties, "kept herself out there," and so forth. With or without Doug. They'd never actually talked about it, but she knew he understood; that's how closely and intuitively connected they were. And it's not like he didn't go without her to Burning Man.

I am so damn lucky, Lola thought woozily, feeling soothing heat from Doug's hand. She was floating on a cloud of exhaustion so thick she couldn't even feel the bumps on the road. I have Doug, and I'm not dead.

As the cab slowed to a stop, Lola began to calculate the number of feet remaining between the car and her bed.

"Hey, monkey, don't forget your ba—" Doug started, but he didn't have to. Right then, her cell phone vibrated so hard her giant bag jumped.

Lola dug for it madly, hoping to find it before the actual ringing kicked in. She really wasn't up for any shrill noises right now, especially not the theme from *Mork & Mindy*. Note to self, thought Lola: no more "ironic" ring tones.

She flipped open the phone, assuming it was Annabel. But her caller ID read "Unknown."

Hmm. Must be Detective Bobbsey, calling to say he nabbed Reading Guy and got a full confession and Quentin is free to go.

"Hello?"

"Lola?" Hmm. A detective would call her Ms. Somerville.

"Mmmhmm?" She started to get out of the cab. Doug was paying.

"It's Quentin."

"Oh, Quentin!" Lola dropped her bag and switched ears. "Quentin. I am so sorry. I don't even know what to—"

"Me neither, Lola, me neither." Lola heard voices and a metallic clang.

"Quentin, where are you?"

Doug closed the door and the cab sped off, its Available light fading futilely over the canal bridge and into the distance. He folded his arms and listened. The hazy half moon seemed to be tilting down and listening, too.

"On a pay phone at the police station."

"Really? God, they should let you go home! They really think you can help them?"

"Sort of."

"What do you mean?"

"Well, I feel like they really think *I* did it."

"You are fucking kidding me." I know it's "always the boyfriend," Lola thought. But not *this* boyfriend.

"What!?" Doug mouthed.

"Hang on." Lola put a hand over the receiver and said, "They think he did it!"

"Who, Reading Guy?" asked Doug.

"No no no, Quentin!" said Lola.

"No way," said Doug.

"I know!" said Lola. "It just doesn't—" Doug motioned to her phone.

"Sorry, Quentin," she said. "So what's the deal? Is this, like, your one phone call or something?" Lola asked.

"Lola, I need your help."

"Well, of course, Quentin." Of course. If I hadn't set you up with Mimi, you wouldn't be miserable or under suspicion right now. I owe you. Big time. "Do you need help finding a lawyer? I have my Palm right here." Lola reached for her bag, which sat between a peony and some lemon verbena. Oh wait, my Palm is *in* my phone. Forgot. Technology.

"No, yeah, I called a lawyer, thanks. Guy from my biking club," said Quentin. "But what I want you to do"—his voice dropped to a whisper—"might not be legal."

"Might not be legal?" asked Lola. "You want me to marry a woman?"

"Heh, no," said Quentin.

"You know I'd do just about anything for you right now, but—"

Doug smiled slightly, perhaps feeling a tad superior. He knew about the mouse.

"—but I have to tell you, my crime-fighting—not to mention my crime-committing days—are over," said Lola.

Before she and Doug had started dating, they had bent a few laws in the process of helping expose what had turned out to be a bigger-than-Hallmark conspiracy involving their former employer. Through that experience, Lola had learned, first and foremost, that Doug was the kind of guy who both calls himself a feminist *and* enjoys a good high-speed car chase: just her type. She had also confirmed beyond a doubt that her childhood obsessions with Harriet the Spy and Encyclopedia Brown—and, yes, the Hardys, the Bobbseys, and of course Miss Drew—to the exclusion of most other preadolescent literature, had paid off; she, like her young adult literary idols, was actually pretty good at blowing covers and solving whodunits. That type of skill showed not only in *Pink Slip* but also in the investigative journalism pieces she didn't feel editors assigned her often enough, even though she'd won a lefty media watchdog award for her article proving that the leak about the guy who totally didn't kill JonBenét Ramsey had come from inside the Beltway.

"What I need you to do, well, I don't think it's a giant deal, crime-wise," Quentin was saying. "But it might be a big deal to me. And Lola, I'm barely holding it together as it is." He was clearly near tears.

Doug was gesturing. *Can we go inside?* Lola had practically forgotten they were on the sidewalk, under a dark gray sky—it's never quite night in New York—and the wan glow of the streetlights.

Lola nodded, walking and talking. She and Doug climbed the metal-grate steps to the front door. "Okay, Quentin," she said warily. "I'm listening."

Five

Doug was adamant. "I'm not letting you go in there alone," he insisted.

"Into Quentin's apartment?" Lola asked, frowning.

"No, into his Mac."

They were leaning on their kitchen counter, knocking around what Quentin had explained to Lola.

"Want some?" Lola was firing up the stainless steel coffeemaker with a timer and built-in grinder. (Wedding present.) "Wait, what am I saying? No Peet's for you," she said. "You're going to bed."

It was well after midnight. Lola would have loved Doug's company on her mission, but she truly thought it unnecessary. While Doug was the night owl, Quentin was her friend. Plus, it's always nice to be needed, and to take any chance to prove that you and your husband aren't joined at the hip. Besides, at least *one* of them should get some sleep.

While the coffee began burbling, Lola got out the travel mug and sat down on a barstool. Since their three parents had generously helped with the down payment on the apartment—Doug's dad, a widower in Los Alamos, held a lucrative patent on something having to do with solar cars—the couple had opted to put their remaining wedding gift cash toward what they'd agreed was the most important room: the kitchen. (Doug had honed his amateur chef skills at the side of his big sister, who ran a country restaurant near Glacier National Park that had its own cookbook. Lola had honed her eating skills in their apartment.)

The kitchen's best features, other than the refrigerated leftovers, were the granite countertops, wooden cabinets painted in a purple and lime patchwork, and a light fixture Lola had fashioned from a colander in a brief fit of crafting. A smaller one made with a cheese grater hung over the flea market diner-style breakfast table. A counter, with barstools, separated the kitchen from the L-shaped area that served as living and dining room; this allowed Doug—in theory—to simmer his famous gnocchi while chatting with guests on the couch. In theory, that is, because *if* guests actually made the trek to NoWay, they always hung out in the kitchen to begin with. Which was partly because their living room was still a little bit "grad student," as Lola called it: steamer-trunk coffee table, bulging bookcases—Lola had never been able to achieve that spare "intersperse your artfully displayed books with framed photos and interesting *objets* from your travels" look—and a vaguely funky floor lamp from Target whose on/off knob had been missing since the day after they bought it.

Lola and Doug did their own second-best hanging out in their shared office, decorated with vintage photos of their shared idols, Johnny Cash and Dolly Parton, though more often than not, Doug was out with clients doing his mysterious "strategic new media consulting." Some of their most memorable conversations took place with the two of them seated back-to-back at their desks, not even turning their heads from their work while they bantered. Many of said conversations took place over instant messenger.

Doug took some seltzer out of the stainless steel fridge, which Lola still couldn't believe she was grown-up enough to own. The seltzer, they got delivered; every two weeks the guy—last guy in

the borough still in the business—rattled up in his truck filled
with wooden crates of siphon-topped blue glass bottles. When
Lola had mentioned the Last Seltzer Man to her dad, his eyes
had misted over with childhood memories of a Canarsie much
changed. The guy with the umbrellaed cart holding a block of
ice and jouncing bottles of flavored syrups: he, she assured her
father, still came around during the summer.

Doug poured himself and Lola each a glass of seltzer. Lola felt
the chilly fizz land on her hand. "Listen, Lo, at least take backup,"
he said.

"C'mon, hon, I'll really be okay."

"No, I mean my mini–hard drive. You shouldn't go around
deleting willy-nilly without backing up."

"Good idea. Will do," said Lola. "Bedtime snack?" Lola gestured toward a white bakery bag and the dedicated bagel toaster.
(Wedding present.) "There's garlic and rye."

Doug sighed. "Just be careful, okay?" He took some Gruyere
out of the fridge and grabbed a $75 cheese knife with a special
pointy nose like a spiny lobster. (They had each brought one to
the marriage. Kismet.)

"I totally will. And, sweetie, will you call me a car service?"
Cabs didn't just cruise Brooklyn. To leave the borough, you had to
really want to.

Quentin had explained to Lola that the cops would be taking
him home in the next while. That was the good news. "You
wouldn't mind if I looked around a little when we drop you off,
would you?" Bobbsey had asked.

"I couldn't say no!" Quentin told Lola. "It's not like I have
anything to hide."

"Of course not," Lola had said.

"Except I do."

"Talk."

"Okay," Quentin said. "You know how crossword puzzles have themes?"

"Yeah, of course."

"Well, the one I'm right in the middle of writing?"

"Yeah?"

"Well, the theme of this one?"

"Uh-huh?"

"Is famous murderers."

"Oh," said Lola.

"Yeah," said Quentin.

"What's a seven-letter word for 'It just doesn't look good'?" asked Lola.

"So just go ahead and delete the entire Documents folder," said Quentin.

"I-M-H-O-S-E-D!" Lola exclaimed.

"What?" asked Quentin.

"Never mind," said Lola. "But wait. The whole Documents folder? Isn't that a little excessive?" asked Lola. "Wouldn't deleting the Vaguely Incriminating Crosswords folder be sufficient?

"It's fine. I don't need any of that stuff, really, and I don't want to take any chances," said Quentin. "Anyway, the doorman, he's a stand-up guy. Used to be a woman who filled in on overnights, didn't know her very well, but now she's only once a week because she's writing a book about being a lady doorman, I think, or something. Anyway, the guy and I, we're close. Just say my name, and he'll let you in. And Lola, could you hurry? Cops said they still have to do a bunch of paperwork first, but still."

"On it," said Lola. "Just one thing, Quentin. Why me?"

Quentin sighed. "Well, given everything that happened to you before with Ovum, and then your book, and that other investigative stuff you've done, I figured you were always up for a caper. You've got skillz, as they say!"

"Thanks," said Lola. Doug did call her "incident-prone." And it was always nice to feel a little indispensable.

"That's *skillz* with a *z*," noted Quentin. "Plus . . ."

"Uh-huh? . . ."

"Well, it's getting late, and—"

"Uh-huh . . ."

"Well, you're still freelancing, right?"

"Yes . . ." Lola knew where this was going.

"I was also thinking you don't, like, *have to* get up in the morning. So I felt less bad about—"

"Oooookay, Quentin, I'm totally on it. Don't worry about a thing. I'll check in with you soon."

I actually do have to get up in the morning, thank you very much, thought Lola. Just because I do it wearing my giant tomato slippers doesn't mean it's not a job.

At that moment, something gave Lola the vague feeling that she did have something specific to do tomorrow morning, something that did in fact require shoes, but she couldn't place it.

Anyway. She had to hurry.

Six

"Mom, it's the middle of the night!"

"Why didn't you answer your home phone, Lulu?"

"Because it's the middle of the night!"

"But then why did you answer your cell phone?"

"I heard both ring, so I figured it was something important," Lola offered. She was an old hand at not giving her mother more information than she needed—for example, the fact that she was currently speeding uptown to tamper with evidence at a young man's apartment, in which she had once slept.

"Are you sure you're okay, Lulu? Do you want me to get on the shuttle?"

"Yes, Mom. I mean, no. I mean, yes, I'm okay, no, no shuttle, thank you," Lola said. "How did you hear about Mimi so fast, any-way?"

"Well, I couldn't sleep—and now I see why!—so I got on the online."

Her befuddled terminology notwithstanding, Mrs. Somerville had actually gotten pretty handy with the Internet. As far as Lola was concerned, her mother and the World Wide Web were a match made in hell. Lola remembered the good old days—when the newspaper clippings about preliminary studies showing a link between cell phones and brain tumors, or which types of fish have the most mercury contamination, would arrive, nice and slow, by U.S. mail.

"Let me see what else is on the Google," said Mrs. Somerville. Clickety-click, Lola heard.

Lola was an only child. She got a lot of attention. Which she loved, except when she didn't. The only phase when she'd ever really wanted a sibling—specifically, an older brother who'd tousle her hair and explain what the "bases" were—had occurred when she was too young to realize that what she actually wanted was a boyfriend. Lola did know, however, that more siblings had been wanted: when she was little, her parents—a medical professional and a professor of neurolinguistics, and therefore not the type to use terms such as "wee-wee" or "daddy plants a seed"—had given her way too much information about whose plumbing had gone wrong where, and why it looked like it was just going to be the three of them.

At that moment, it had occurred to young Lola, if subconsciously, that she was going to have to work extra hard to make Mom and Dad not sad that she, just she, was all they had.

Her mother, Audrey, was a registered nurse and social worker, so, to be fair, fussing was her job. Interestingly and refreshingly, though, Mrs. Somerville had generally steered clear of interfering in Lola's love life; somehow she'd seemed less worried about Lola's getting married than she was about Lola's getting melanoma. Perhaps this raise-an-independent-daughter spirit stemmed back to Mrs. Somerville's days as a collaborating writer on *Our Bodies, Our Selves*. Lola's childhood had been very *Free to Be You and Me*, only with more hand washing.

"Hey, Mom, can I go now?" Lola asked. "I'm really trying to get eight hours tonight, as recommended in that article you sent me about sleep and toxoplasmosis."

"Lulu!" Mrs. Somerville sounded freshly upset.

"What, Mom?"

"*You* found the body?"

"Mom, what are you reading?" Is there *anything* Doug can rig up to keep my mother off the Web? That would give *parental control* a whole new meaning.

"*Royalty*," said Audrey. *Royalty*?! thought Lola. That my mother knows about it is either a testament to its market penetration or to her omniscience or both. "It's right here, under 'Breaking.' Oh, this—*this* is just too much. Lola, you have got to be more careful!"

"I'll try not to stumble on any more bodies, Mom, I promise."

"Not with corpses, with reporters. This Page Proof person spelled your name wrong."

Oh, for God's sake. At least Wally's pseudonym wouldn't trigger any memories from the Aunt Fern fix-up.

"Just promise me you're okay, Lulu?"

"I promise, Mommy."

"Try not to go out."

"At all?"

"Well, I suppose daytime is still okay."

"I'll do my best," said Lola.

"If you promise to wear a helmet," said Mrs. Somerville. "Kidding! Now let's both try to get some sleep—that is, as soon as I give the ombudsman an earful."

"Mom, blogs don't have—"

"I know, Lola."

Lola laughed. I really oughta give her some more credit. "Good night, Mom."

"Good night, Lulu."

"I'm going up to feed Quentin Frye's cat!" Lola waved cheerily at the doorman. Never mind that Quentin was allergic to cats, not to mention dogs—yet another reason he and Lola could never be together—or that it was the middle of the night.

The doorman looked up, startled, from his Sudoku. Lola hadn't realized he'd nodded off. "Morning!" he said, waving her in.

Piece of cake. Quentin hadn't mentioned that the doorman, much like the building, was prewar. In his case, Peloponnesian, Lola figured. She headed through the lobby.

"Excuse me, miss?"

Uh-oh.

She turned to face the doorman, sure he'd realized he'd just waved in a complete stranger under utterly false pretenses, sure he was about to tell her to take a hike.

"I mean, ma'am?"

Oh, God. How matronly do I look?

"Yes, sir?" Act casual.

"Wondering if you could do me a favor, while you're on your way up there?"

Phew. "Of course!"

"Stray piece of mail for Mr. Frye." He held out a white windowed business envelope and looked at her with rheumy eyes. "Mind leaving it for him?"

"Not at all," said Lola. She slipped the envelope into her bag.

"Much obliged, ma'am," said the doorman, touching the brim of his dusty doorman cap.

I so love that he just said "much obliged" and tipped his cap, Lola thought. So much so that I'm over the "ma'am" part.

She smiled and waved and headed down the hall, her mission back under way.

Lola remembered both this place and her singlehood in their faded glory. The small apartment building was the type where your first therapist, the one you had when you still wanted someone "nice" and validating, would have had her office: thick but worn beige carpeting, lovely mahogany detailing that needed a touch-up ten years ago, one of those teeny rickety elevators with an accordion door like a child's safety gate. The security camera, though, that was new. Times change.

Following Quentin's instructions, Lola found his bike in the first-floor storage room where all the tenants kept theirs. Quentin was one of those serious bicyclists who ride around Central Park in long slim groups like schools of fish. He kept an extra key duct-taped under the seat—no doubt Mimi's idea. Poor head-in-the-clouds Quentin; his apartment door evidently locked automatically behind you, usually at the very moment you realized you'd forgotten your key.

Poor Mimi, for that matter.

Lola eased herself into Quentin's apartment. She had forgotten how nice it was. What's a nine-letter-word for *affords on puzzle-writer's salary?* She had no idea. It was all dark paneled wood, like dorm rooms in movies about Yale. It was a two-bedroom—he used one as a study—with a sliver of a kitchen, its beige counters nearly bare. There was a public-radio-logo umbrella in a stand by the door, right next to the canvas man-bag Lola was looking for.

She plopped on the bed—which, in the middle of the night, was more enticing than the desk chair—with Quentin's iBook, musing that, after six months of marriage, the whole dating thing seemed at once very far and very near away. On the one hand, she could no longer fathom waking up in any bed but her own or do-ing the toothpaste-on-her-finger brush of shame—though she had always half-enjoyed the challenge of tracking down an Ameri-cano and a decent muffin in whatever neighborhood she'd woken up in. On the other—and the thought made her smile as she waited for the computer to fire up—sometimes she'd momentarily "forget" that she was married, and when Doug called for whatever reason, she'd get that *he called!* bloop in her tummy. The bloop was dormant, evidently, but not dead. Which, hey, was nice.

Okay, here goes.

You know, I'll just do Quentin a favor and back up his whole hard drive, considering that Doug's state-of-the-art bionic mini-drive holds like a billion gigs.

Now for the Documents file. Trash. Empty trash. Mission accomplished.

Lola hit Shut Down. This would have taken me an hour in Windows, Lola thought, and Doug would be proud of me for thinking that. She scanned the room for her shoes.

Rrrring!

Lola jumped. Her phone.

"Can't sleep," said Annabel.

"Me neeth," said Lola. She quickly explained where she was, pacing the room. "So I really can't talk. Oh but wait, just tell me quick, where'd you guys go after Cabin 9?" she asked Annabel.

"Well, Leo dropped me off—"

"Ever the gentleman."

"And then Darius called."

"Oh!" said Lola. Darius. The rug trader. He was actually *from* Casablanca, which, until Annabel met him, Lola had forgotten was a place you could actually be from.

"He intoxicates me," said Annabel.

"I'll bet," said Lola.

"As in, he gets me drunk."

"Ah," said Lola. She'd wandered into the study. A couple of crossword drafts lay on Quentin's desk. Better grab these, too, she thought.

". . . which will make the nightmares I'm going to have about Mimi even worse," Annabel finished.

"I know, Bella. I know. But let me call you from the cab before the cops show up and find me here and I have to do some sort of *I Love Lucy* stunt to escape?"

"Okay. Mwah."

"Mwah."

I was so wired a second ago, thought Lola. Now I'm tired. Crap.

Sleepy.

I am not my best after ten PM. And now it's even after ten PM in California.

I know, thought Lola, I'll just look at this crossword for a second. Right over there on the bed. Huh. I should really know what *silicates* are, shouldn't I? Five letters. See, doing the crossword will make me think it's morning. And then I'll get right up and go, like I do in the—

Lola heard a noise. In her dream, it was the penguins, who were about to come in from the yard with Madonna. One took a key out from somewhere beneath its feathers. Lola heard it turning in the lock.

She heard it in real life, too.

Lola was an early sleeper, but also—fortunately—a light one.

Stop, drop, and roll.

She was under the bed in less than two seconds.

Seven

There was a slipper in her face, the kind the dog brings Dad after work. Avuncular, elbow-patch-wearing Quentin was ahead of his time.

The door closed. Silence. Lola waited, trying to do some sort of out-only yoga breathing so that she wouldn't inhale whatever it was that accumulates under the bed of even the tidiest single male. Besides ex-girlfriends.

Lola heard footsteps but no voices. *God, if they would just speak, I could gauge their whereabouts more precisely and plan my Lucy maneuver.* The bedroom was at the far end of the living room, with the door open, so if she came out, she'd be visible.

They were coming closer. Lola held what was left of her breath.

Clonk. The side of her head slammed into the floor, as the bottom of the bed had just slammed into her head.

Hold on.

"Quentin?"

"Aaaaaah!"

Lola rolled out from under. Quentin was crouched at the head of his bed, pillow raised to strike.

"Lola?!"

"No, a giant mouse."

"Not funny."

"I'm sorry," said Lola. Jeez, Somerville, this guy's girlfriend was just murdered. Once in a while, would it kill you—er, once in a while, could you *not* make a joke?

Lola gave Quentin a giant hug. "I mean, I'm really sorry."

"Thanks." Quentin was stiff in her arms. Still shocked and numb, surely.

"So wait," Lola said, sitting back. "After all that, they just dropped you off?"

"I guess," shrugged Quentin. "Maybe they were just trying to intimidate me."

"Probably," said Lola. God *damn.* This Nervous Nellie totally eek-a-moused me again, thought Lola. Boy, should I have known.

"Lola, thanks," said Quentin.

"Don't mention it," said Lola. Let it go, Somerville. "Listen, you really shouldn't be alone. Do you want me to stay around, you know, wait until you fall asleep or whatever?" Oh, it's so nice to be married. You can say stuff like that without sounding suspect.

"Thanks, Lola, I'm good," Quentin said. "My sister's on her way over right now from her shift at the ER."

"I can wait."

"No really, I'm fine," said Quentin. "I'll call you tomorrow. If you don't mind."

"Of course not," said Lola. Genuine sadness and lingering guilt swirled inside her again. I really shouldn't leave until his sister gets here, thought Lola, though she needed her bed badly. "Let me at least get you something to drink."

Quentin accepted a glass of flat Pellegrino—the only thing in his fridge besides batteries and a crusty two-ounce jar of artisanal wasabi—and took a sip.

"I guess her parents will let me know about the funeral. I hope

they will. Would be nice to have met them under better circumstances."

"I know, Quentin," Lola said, sincere sorrow in her voice.

"Lola," Quentin asked, "who would want to do this to Mimi?"

"I don't know, Quentin."

"You don't?"

"No, I really—wait, what do you mean?"

"I just thought *Lola Somerville* would have a bead on this somehow," said Quentin. "You seem to always be in the middle of
things."

"Sure, if by *always* you mean that one time two years ago."

"Well, you did find Mimi's body." Quentin's voice caught.

Fair point. "But not on purpose," said Lola. "And unfortunately, the killer wasn't included."

"I'll bet you could find him," said Quentin.

"Quentin, I—"

"I mean that as a compliment but also a statement of fact,"
said Quentin. "And also, I guess, a request."

"But—" Lola didn't know where to start. "What about the
police? The detective seemed on top of things."

"Sure, until the next orange alert," Quentin said. "They'll be all
over it tomorrow—and it'll be all over the *Day*, naturally—but then
they'll be back to human-shielding the Statue of Liberty."

Even earnest Quentin had reason to be cynical. These days,
the blue line was stretched thinner than ever. And on top of it all,
there was the Penelope effect. Penelope—one name was all she
needed—was the omnipotent single-named domestic goddess/pop
singer/movie actress/anti–land mine activist/talk show host with
whom Lola had crossed paths quite closely during the Ovum incident. On her top-rated, drop-everything, taste-making TV show,
Penelope!, authors regularly broke down in tears and admitted
to substantial fabrications in their "memoirs." Back in the day,
one offhand comment by Penelope on the air had resulted in a

nationwide shortage of vegetable peelers. Another, more significantly, had caused Internet stocks to plummet, leading directly to the dot-com bust. And, more recently, ever since Penelope had devoted a show to race differences in law enforcement and media attention to murder cases, the police and the papers had been making a big show of devoting fewer resources to the murders of pretty white girls.

"Also," Quentin went on, "I just don't trust the police. One time my bike seat was stolen outside that bar, what's it called, where they have the strip spelling bee? The cops, I am telling you, did not want to lift a finger!"

"They were probably more interested in watching to see if some hot girl had to spell *chthonian*."

"You know, I've never heard that word actually pronounced before," said Quentin.

"I have," sighed Lola. "Doug's a gamer."

"So I don't know, maybe you could at least nose around a little, somewhere, somehow?" asked Quentin.

"Quentin, I'm not a detective." I really, *really* owe him one, but murder? For the life of me, I have no clue where to start. I would be insane to take this on.

"I know," said Quentin. "Not officially. But come on. The whole thing at Ovum, those articles you've written—you've busted your share of bad guys." He accepted some more Pellegrino. "And I'd just—I'd feel so much better if I knew you were looking into it. You just have such a good sense of, I don't know, people. Their motives. I feel like you can really get inside people's heads."

Oh, man. He's really not letting up. "Quentin," Lola pulled her hair back into ponytail position and then let it drop. "You and I dated for like ten minutes. We e-mail every three months. All you really know about me is that I'm not scared of dead mice, I'm bad with the names of rivers in Eastern Europe and I fit under your bed. Where are you drawing all these conclusions?"

"I can just tell," Quentin said. "You know, from all the characters you developed so brilliantly in your book."

He read my book?

He used the word *brilliant*?

Lola caught herself. No, Quentin, no! she thought. Stop flattering me! If you continue, I may actually say yes! Quit it!

"Speaking of which," said Quentin, "I don't know, maybe if you find the guy first, you can write a book about it."

Hold on. Lola's mouth twitched, threatening to smile. Quentin Frye was no Jodie Foster. But he was, in effect, *calling her with a book idea.*

Lola looked down at the floor, then up at the ceiling. Her guilt and her ego did a high five. "Okay, Quentin," said Lola. "I'll see what I can do."

When Quentin's twin sister, Penny, arrived, Lola got ready to leave. Blond, with wire-framed glasses and maroon Dansko clogs, Penny was still in her white coat from work. Since when did we all get old enough to be doctors? Lola thought.

"Say, Lola, can I ask your advice sometime?" asked Penny.

"Sure," said Lola. "Intubate."

Penny laughed. "No, about writing. I'm working on a book proposal."

Who the hell isn't?

"Of course," said Lola. "Anytime."

Much as she felt surrounded, oppressed, by people with book ideas, Lola felt safe in the knowledge that Penny would never finish her proposal, much less publish the book. That was how the universe maintained literary equilibrium: everyone *thought* they had a book in them, but few realized what it took to get one down on paper. She looked back into the apartment. "Quentin, are you going to be okay?"

"Eventually," he said. "And Lola, thanks for everything."

Lola hailed a cab. She rested a hand on her chin and watched Second Avenue's trattorias and nail salons go by. Where was that muffin place? They had a solid apple-ginger, if she remembered correctly. Right around here, no? Yes, that kiosk definitely looked famliar. It was right—nope. The muffin place was now a cell phone store.

"Annabel? We're old."

"Not too old to be blabbing on the phone in the middle of the night," said Annabel.

"Right! That's exactly my point," said Lola. She was now lying down, seat beltless, on the backseat of the cab. If an accident didn't kill her, her mother would. "We are old, but we don't act it. I didn't pack away Giraffe until my wedding night, for God's sake." Giraffe had been Lola's stuffed companion since childhood.

"You made air holes in the box, right?" asked Annabel.

"Yes, and I also put in some leaves," said Lola. "But I mean, pretty much all my high school and college friends are, you know, grown-ups. Remember that party we went to when you came home with me at Christmas?"

"Yeah, at what's-her-name's," said Annabel. "Their place was so grown-up I totally thought they were house-sitting."

"Right? They had those little brass lamps over their art."

"They had a fucking *den*."

Lola and Annabel paused, letting the full weight of that memory—and that word—sink in.

"Part of that is having money," said Lola. "But God, people our age are doctors. Lawyers. Mayors. Hockey moms."

"Corpses."

"Right."

"Just trying to lighten things up," said Annabel.

Lola gave a grim chuckle, then went on. "Even though I'm married, I sometimes still feel like we're really just playing house. Dress-up. Like I'm walking around in my Mom's smeared lipstick and too-big shoes."

"Lo, *I'm* the one who can't even commit to address labels. Not that I necessarily want things to be different. I'm just saying. I relate."

"I know you do, Bella."

What would I do without Annabel? Annabel who actually knew current band names, who carried a Leatherman, who ate only food that was round: Garden Burgers, Krispy Kremes, beer (which counted, she said, if you looked at the bottle from the bottom). Annabel said Lola kept her grounded. Lola said Annabel made sure she reached.

"But seriously, Lo, you're not exactly complaining either, are you?" Annabel asked. "I mean, first of all, you *are* a writer. Your job *is* a *job* job. You're the first one to tell everyone else that," she said. "Nicely, of course."

"No no, I know. I guess I'm just more . . . marveling. Whether or not we feel like adults—"

"—or act like—"

"—or act like adults, I guess . . . it's just amazing that we've gotten to the place in life where what we do is who we are."

Annabel said nothing.

Oof. Lola squeezed her eyes shut, wishing she could take that back. She'd remembered—too late—that, actually, Annabel did not have a defining what-she-does that made her who she was. And the last thing Annabel needed was for Lola to point that out.

"All right, listen," Lola said quickly. "I gotta start giving the driver directions." She could no longer see the tops of buildings from her vantage point, so she must be in Brooklyn. "Bella, thanks. You totally make me feel normal."

"Me, too, Lo," said Annabel. Lola hoped so. "Now get some sleep."

"You, too!" said Lola.

"Naw, I'm good," said Annabel. "I slept last year."

It was alarmingly close to the time Lola usually got up. She'd seen the delivery trucks already making the rounds of soon-to-open coffee shops, leaving paper-bagged bundles of fresh baked goods leaning outside the locked doors. (This was also a sight she hadn't seen since her single days, except for that one time she and Doug had waited in line until 4:30 AM to buy the thirteenth Harry Potter.) It had never ceased to amaze Lola that these bags of sweet treats never got stolen. War, murder, all manner of pain: your world could fall apart at any moment, and yet? Day after day, there were the muffins. The café owners could rely on two things every morning: one, that the sun would rise, and two, that those sweet-smelling sacks of croissants and scones would be waiting for them when they got to work. What, Lola wondered, could possibly be more reassuring?

"You know what, just drop me at this corner, please," she said to the driver. The newspaper trucks were out already, too—and one was pulling up to Lola's local bodega. Though she could barely keep her eyes open, Lola was curious at least to see if Mimi's murder had made the cover of the *Day*.

Lola knew full well, by the way, that she could have checked the *Day*, not to mention *Royalty*, twenty minutes ago using the Web browser on her cell phone, but doing so would have put some holes in her argument with Doug that no one needed a freaking Web browser on their cell phone.

"Thanks," she said, shelling out twenties for the driver. With what they'd spent on transportation that night, she and Doug could buy two more cheese knives.

The *New York Day* truck driver dropped a twine-wrapped stack by the blue wire racks outside the bodega door. Lola looked down at the five-inch-tall headline.

Murder-Tini

Oh, for God's sake.

As Lola stared down, two feet stepped into her view. Two feet wearing ratty black sneakers. Two feet she'd recently seen running.

Without raising her head, Lola looked up through her lashes.

It was Reading Guy.

Eight

Lola thought immediately of those signs at Yosemite at which she and Doug had once laughed nervously: "If confronted by a mountain lion, do not run, as this may trigger its instinct to attack. Instead, back off slowly." Or something like that. Lola backed away from the sneakers without making eye contact and set off briskly toward home, deliberately jingling her keys as if to say, "Back off, Reading Guy! My mom just forwarded me an e-mail about someone who saved her own life by using her mailbox key to gouge an attacker's Adam's apple."

Or, wait. Shit. Was that it? Or were you supposed to run *toward* the mountain lion?

Lola glanced behind her, covering the move by pretending to scratch her ear with her shoulder. No one. Too late.

Should I call Bobbsey? And tell him what? That I happened to see the same oddball in two places, and at no point did he move toward or threaten me in any way?

Lola reached her garden. A clematis vine had sprung from its trellis, reaching across her way like a bony arm.

No, she thought, I'm gonna keep this to myself. Remember, I'm supposed to be helping Quentin by knowing stuff the cops don't, and remember, I'm supposed to be solving the mystery and turning it into a book. Kind of the way that woman did, the one who talked her kidnapper out of kidnapping her by reading him the Zone Diet, or some such? Or did we later find out that she was saved not so much by the soothing words of Barry Sears but by the fact that she gave her attacker crystal meth? Anyway. That lady was plucky. And, of course, she's now totally writing a book.

Lola wrapped the stray vine back around a stake and tiptoed inside.

Uch, of course. My brave "escape" from the guy who was clearly not chasing me made me come home without the damn paper.

There's always the online, she thought.

No. It's so freaking late. Get to bed, Somerville. Whatever you do, do not turn on the computer.

Lola fired up her Mac.

Publishing Biz to Perp: We Meant "Cutthroat" As a Metaphor
Sadly, Not Your Usual *Royalty* Party Report
Posted by Page Proof

Acclaimed and adorable chick lit author Mimi McKee, 31, was found mysteriously murdered at her own party, a celebration of the publication of her novel *Gay Best Friend* at the ultratrendy Bowery watering hole, Cabin 9. Coquettish and comely even in death, she lay in a rarely used basement storage closet, her stylish wrap dress revealing just hints of ivory thigh and décolletage. Ms. McKee's throat had been viciously slashed with a broken cocktail glass.

Could the weapon of choice be a nod to the beverage of choice of the typical chick in McKee's genre of lit? Police declined to say, noting that the killer was still at large. "I assure you, we'll get the guy. And by 'get' I mean 'nab,' not marry," said police detective Bradley Bobbsey, who admitted to being an aficionado of the promising young writer's work.

Reached at home late at night in Mexico, Maine, Ms. McKee's distraught parents declined to be interviewed. A relative said only that the burial would be private.

Others who knew McKee were shocked to hear that she fell victim to a violent crime. "She's was just such a sweet all-American girl," said McKee's third-grade teacher, Priscilla Wren, roused from slumber by the shocking news. "I still have the note she wrote me about how much she loved the hot dog stands everywhere in New York, because they made it so easy to buy food for homeless people."

McKee's seemingly unthreatening boyfriend, Quentin Frye, was questioned and later released.

The body of Ms. McKee was discovered—too late—by partygoer Lila Summerville, who appeared to have been wandering, confused, in the basement. Ms. Summerville claimed to be a fellow "writer," but her "books" did not appear on a search of Amazon.com.

What the—?

Told you you should have gone to bed, thought Lola.

Ping! Instant message from Annabel. She was still up, too?

"Oy, SORRY," Annabel typed. "Saw the article. At least he got your name wrong?"

"SLEEP!" typed Lola.

"XOXOXO!" typed Annabel.

"ZZZZZZZ!" typed Lola.

Lola closed her computer and tiptoed into the bedroom, stopping on the way to peel her contact lenses out of her sore eyes. The room was perfectly still, with not so much as a breeze whispering through the curtains that Lola had paid a nice Italian lady to make, which was the kind of business you could still, if you knew where to look, get done in Brooklyn. She tossed her clothes on the floor and climbed into bed with Doug. He was sleeping on his back with his knees up, which Lola found bizarre and adorable, though it made her have to trade spooning for a sleeping still life more like fish knifing.

I don't know how to solve a murder, thought Lola. I can't dust for fingerprints. I'm not even like Doug, who figures out the ending of *CSI: Dead Model* in the first ten minutes. What was I thinking? What have I done?

She rolled over. Her eye caught the stack of books on her nightstand, bathed in the faint yellowish glow of her family hand-me-down clock radio, a clunky vintage model with an analog face.

I am never going to finish *Anna Karenina*.

But you know what? Books. That's what I've got that they don't. They know blood spatter patterns, but I know Mimi's world. That's gotta count for something. Plus, I recall very clearly from Encyclopedia Brown that a person's reflection appears upside down in a spoon. You never know when that could come up.

Anyway. Tomorrow.

Lola shifted onto her back, her left shoulder touching Doug's right. She took a deep breath and closed her eyes.

Just. Need. To. Sleep. On. This.

Her alarm went off.

Nine

Hell's Bells.

"... and with a $1000 pledge, Garrison Keillor will leave the outgoing message on your answering machine," said NPR.

"Grplnah," said Doug.

That wasn't even a catnap, thought Lola. Not even a bird nap. Not even an ant nap.

Doug rolled over. "Sweetie, go back to sleep," he said, eyes closed.

Catnap.

Dogs.

Lola leapt out of bed.

"Wish I could," she said, kissing Doug on the nose. "Looks like you're sleeping for two."

Fifteen minutes later, after prodding her contact lenses from their own brief rest, wrestling her hair into a ponytail, and giving her garden a quick bare-minimum spritz, Lola was sipping a blue-and-white paper cup of crappy bodega coffee—whole milk, one sugar—as she crossed the girdered bridge over the canal. An orange sun, pale and round as a canned peach, was just beginning to cast its muted light. The air still carried a bit of a damp chill; Lola was glad she had grabbed her light cotton jacket and also that she, a big believer in breakfast, had thought to stick in its pocket a couple of Fig Newtons.

Lola shot an appreciative glance at one of her favorite features of the canal: a rickety red caboose-shaped structure topped with a huge bin full of stones, perched on the bank like a giant square pelican. The faded sign read Lundy Crushers, which, not coincidentally, was also the name of the borough's women's roller derby team. Ever wonder where rocks come to get crushed into gravel? Here's where. There are whole worlds out there—out here—that most of us never think about, Lola mused.

Her only company was one seagull, who landed on the railing and stared at her sideways as she passed. This is why I am a morning person, thought Lola. Even if I haven't slept. Now's when I can think.

Thank goodness she had remembered: today was the day she'd promised to dog-sit for Daphne Duplex. Thirty seconds of sleep notwithstanding, Lola was trying—with measured success—to convince herself that having to dog-sit today was a good thing.

Daphne, successful author of *So Many Men, So Little Taste*, lived about ten blocks away, on the "good" side of the canal. She'd been wise enough to buy her apartment several years earlier, so she was now sitting pretty in a renovated row house at the end of the kind of street that was called a Place. An abandoned warehouse nearby was set to become an Organic Depot. There was talk of moving the New York Giants into a stadium complex to be built over toward Brooklyn Navy Yard, but the plan was being viciously protested by neighborhood activists who had nobler notions of community development (but whose sports experience, frankly, was limited to hot yoga). These people were particularly angry—and fair enough, given that many of them had been driven out of Manhattan when Hamilton Fish Town, the East Village's storied affordable housing complex, had been razed to make way for a Wal-Mart.

Daphne had called Lola just yesterday morning—which now seemed like an eon ago—with an emergency on her hands.

"Hallo, Lola, it's Daphne Duplex. Got your cell from your book publicist, hope to death you're not sore."

Ex-publicist. "Mind? I'm just glad she still has my number."

"Oh, you *are* a stitch," said Daphne. "But say, Lola, I'm in a bit of a pickle. I was wondering if you could do a gal a terribly big favor. I'm on the last day of my book tour here in—let's see, if it's Wednesday, it must be St. Louis—and it seems my regular dogsitter has discovered that her new fella's allergic to bassets. She insists she can't stay another day."

"With the boyfriend?"

"You raise an excellent point, but no. With the pooches. Would you be a peach and pop over tomorrow?"

Does she think I don't work?

More times than she could count, Lola had told someone she was a writer, only to hear, "I'm so jealous! You must get to, like, go to the park all day and journal."

Then again, of course, Daphne was now a work-at-home writer, too—though that was a recent development. The etiquette column she'd written for a now-defunct Web magazine had outlived its parent, unlike the once-popular online advice column that Lola wrote before and during her stint at the ill-fated Ovum. But then a fancy agent had called Daphne and said, "Love your column. Do you think there's a book in there?" Said Daphne: "I do now."

At least that's how Daphne had told the tale, twisting her trademark pink scarf, to a rapt audience of pals, including Lola and Annabel, over cocktails. "Bella?" Lola had whispered. "Can you please go get me a rage-tini?"

But even if my time *is* more flexible than other people's, which admittedly it is, I need more of it for me, thought Lola. I'm not as tireless as I used to be, nor—more importantly—as desperate to please.

Lola's big plan for her thirties, all two of them so far, was to "put herself first," like all the magazines said she should. It was time, she had recently declared, to stop trying to be all things to all people—all people, of course, being emotional extensions of Audrey and Morris Somerville—and to start focusing on numero uno, and numero uno's career. Oh, and numero uno's marriage. Right. Shit.

All of which means, Lola had resolved, that I really must learn to start saying no.

"So you'll do it?" Daphne asked.

"Sure," said Lola.

As she walked, Lola focused on the upside of dog-sitting, which was to begin with this daybreak visit to the dog run. Lola knew she couldn't skip that; not only would the dogs be desperate to go out at their usual time, but, knowing these dog runs, if she didn't show up with Daphne's pets, someone, someone whose dog no doubt owns some sort of raincoat and four tiny boots, would tattle. But given the dogs' schedule of outings—dog run, walk, dog run, walk, vespers—she'd figured she'd set up shop and work over at Daphne's, where it'd be nice and quiet.

Especially now that I really have some thinking to do, thought Lola. It'd be the follow-up to the thinking she'd been doing in the cab home from Quentin's, which itself followed the thinking she'd been doing ever since her book hadn't turned out to be exactly a runaway bestseller. It had all started off so perfectly those few years ago. That is, the last time she'd solved a mystery, she'd gotten a book deal out of it. Oh, and a husband.

At the time, Lola had become an instant It Girl—her own special-edition Ben & Jerry's flavor, fan mail from Ira Glass, the whole nine—and stayed that way for one It Girl unit of time. Unfortunately, by the time *Pink Slip* was actually published, the public had moved on to the next It, whoever it was, and neither Lola, nor her book, could compete with that. All the buzzing interest in a Lifetime movie about her story, a reality show about her then-upcoming marriage, a Michael Moore tell-all about everything that happened (the producers pitched it as a "fuckyoumentary"), had fizzled and faded. Still, the scattered reviews of *Pink Slip*—including the eleven five-star reader write-ups posted on Amazon.com, nine of which were authored, using various pseudonyms, by Annabel—were overall positive. The book itself, to be fair, was doing okay.

But after all she'd done, all she'd written, all she'd accomplished, just okay was not okay with Lola.

Lola knew she couldn't coast on the past forever. She knew she needed new ideas, a fresh, motivating, identity-reestablishing *raison de writer*, but, for so long, nothing had been forthcoming.

So, Lola had been thinking. Maybe I really was right to say yes to Quentin. Maybe this really is an opportunity. An opportunity to get my mind off petty jealousies and help others. An opportunity to come to the aid of someone who wouldn't have lost his girlfriend if I hadn't found her for him. An opportunity to remember what's truly important and meaningful in life. An opportunity, if I play my cards right, for a new, and even better, book deal.

I am a somewhat good person, thought Lola.

She fished the key out of a planter and opened Daphne's door.

It did not take long for Lola to realize that her day of dog-sitting was not going to offer the kind of opportunity she'd had in mind.

Ten

"Seriously, Annabel, I can't get a freaking thing done."

Lola had come back from the dog run expecting Gibson and Sidecar to be tuckered out from all that running around on their itty stumpy basset legs, long ears dragging like useless brakes. She figured they'd then go ahead and do what dogs do: sleep for the next five hours. The second she'd sat down and turned on Daphne's computer, she'd found out she was wrong.

"Can't stop thinking about Mimi, huh?"

"Can't *start* thinking about Mimi," Lola said. "I have to throw the wombat every three seconds."

"Throw the wombat? Is that what the Brooklyn kids are calling vomiting?" asked Annabel.

"No," laughed Lola, "it's—"

"Wait wait wait. Are you *pregnant?*" asked Annabel.

Lola picked up the wombat chew toy and threw it. The dogs skidded across the kitchen, tripping over their ears. "No, I mean *throw the wombat.*"

Annabel was silent, stuck.

"I'm at Daphne's."

Gibson returned the wombat, head held high. Sidecar followed, ever hopeful. Lola sighed and scratched both their noses. The pair had already destroyed one of Lola's flip-flops, a roll of paper towels, and any hope Lola had of having one productive thought until Daphne came back.

"Oh," said Annabel. "Right."

"This may have been a mistake."

The bassets had spent the morning following Lola around Daphne's fabulous Technicolor apartment, which was chockablock with groovy flea market finds, including a painting positioned to offer a permanent "view" of the Chrysler building, complete with full moon. Lola half-expected Tab Hunter to knock at the door.

When Lola looked away, the dogs barked. When she sat at her computer, they whimpered. When she peed, they stared.

"But you love dogs . . . ?" offered Annabel.

"Yeah, but I don't want to marry them," said Lola.

"Now we know why man and dog are just friends," said Annabel.

Lola laughed wearily.

"Listen, Lo, while you're distracted: I have news," Annabel went on.

"What? About Mimi? What?"

"Well, obviously you know I've been trying to figure out what to do with myself since getting back from rock climbing?"

"Hey, did you get the job at the paintball foundation?"

"No, no, not that . . . you know my blog."

Lola did indeed. Called *The Slackline*, it contained Annabel's witty accounts of her time in Colorado doing volunteer work and dating outdoorsmen—the phase of life she called her "Junior League Abroad." The blog had gained a following among climbers and acrophobes alike. Lola hadn't read as much of it as she'd meant to, which made her feel like an ass.

"Well, I got a call from this editor person at Poncho Books."

Poncho was a hip downtown imprint of Disney-Seagram's, the biggest media conglomerate in history.

"They want you to come work for them?"

"No, no—they want to turn the blog into a book."

Lola threw the wombat.

"I think they're calling that a blook now, but . . . I'm not," said Annabel. "Anyway, also a sitcom."

"Oh, my God."

"And a feature film."

Gibson dropped the wombat on Lola's toe. She picked it up, put it in her own mouth, and bit down, hard.

Eleven

"Lola?"

"Sorry! Sorry. The dogs," said Lola. "*Annabel*. That is *awesome!*"

"Thanks, Lo. I mean, it does kind of feel gross and corporate. But then again, so does what I've been doing: supporting the global domination plan of Cup O'Noodles."

"Hah, right," said Lola.

"Plus, it's so weird," Annabel went on. "I mean, it's not like I was even *trying* to sell it. Or that I even think of myself as, like, an official writer."

Don't remind me, Lola thought.

She knew Annabel was doing her best to show that she hadn't been trying to lap Lola. But her efforts were making things worse. No, she's not an official writer! She's not an official anything! Not to be mean. But come *on*.

Annabel had always succumbed to lust, wander- and otherwise, never staying in one place, or with one guy, for long—and never apologizing for it. She and Lola had met years ago, while both in their twenties, when serving on the volunteer staff at a community kids' fair in a run-down Queens neighborhood. Lola was painting kids' faces; next to her, Annabel, wrapped in scarves, was telling kids' fortunes. "You vill meet a beautiful, eeenteresting stranger," she'd say, inspecting a small palm. "Oh! Is *me*!"

During a lull in the fortune-telling action, Annabel had turned to Lola, bangles jingling.

"So, what'd you do?"

"That last one was Princess Jasmine. So were the nine before that, except for one Darth Maul," sighed Lola, wiping her hands on a piece of musty brown accordion-folded paper towel that reminded her of elementary school. "No one will let me do anyone from Kiss."

"Damn kids," smiled Annabel. "But no, I mean, what'd you do to have to do this?"

"Uh, I signed up," answered Lola, puzzled. "What'd *you* do?"

"Drugs," said Annabel. "After today I'll be done with my six-week community service sentence."

But Annabel had evidently seen an all-new future in her own palm that day. Having done her time, she dropped the drugs but kept up with the good deeds. She would later tell Lola that it was something about how Lola didn't judge her that day—though secretly, silently, sheltered Lola had been shocked—that helped make drugs lose their appeal, helped her lose interest in proving her badassitude. Ever able to talk people into paying her enough to live on, Annabel had gone on to save sea turtles in Mexico, fight the death penalty in Alabama, and teach English to the Hmong in St. Paul (and to quite a few suitors as well).

But it was projects Annabel moved on from, not friends—not Lola. She'd remained loyal to Lola ever since that day at the fair, which they'd left with their faces painted, respectively, as Gene Simmons and The Hamburglar. They were joined at the hip, or, depending on where Annabel was, at the instant message, e-mail, and cell phone.

"Hang on, Lo, let me put you on speaker," said Annabel. Her place in Chinatown was so tiny that she could use the speakerphone anywhere in the entire apartment. Though her kitchen consisted basically of a plug-in hot pot (plus pilsner glasses purloined from various dart-focused bars), and her door buzzer didn't work, Annabel's landlord had recently seen fit to practically double her rent. "Think what it'd cost if it had a closet," he'd snarled.

Lola heard Annabel shout, "Heads up, Sparky!" Must be tossing her keys down to a visitor. Maybe the FedEx guy from last week? ("He absolutely, positively, had to be here overnight," Annabel had explained.)

Lola looked at the computer, opened a new document, and typed, "BE HAPPY FOR HER." She enlarged the letters to take up the whole page. Then bold, then italic. Then red. The dogs whimpered.

Phone cradled to her ear, Lola heard a new male voice. "Hey, Lola! Isn't that the best?" It was Leo. "I know she's been dying to tell you."

Been dying?

How long has she known? How long has *he* known?

Annabel's voice came quickly. "Yeah, I found out just before Mimi's party. Then . . . you know. And last night when you were in the cab, I just didn't . . ." In a rare moment of incertitude, Annabel trailed off.

Lola shoved aside, with all her might, a giant pile of angry thoughts. Gibson and Sidecar, play-snarling, locked their jaws onto the coolest toy around: Lola's other flip-flop. Ignoring them, Lola forced herself to stare at the message on the computer screen.

"Whatever, Annabel, this is just so totally, amazingly excellent," she said. "So what happens next?"

"I UPS all this stuff I sold last week on eBay," said Annabel. "Leo came by on his lunch to help me schlep." Which was the kind of thing Leo did. It was in his nature, and—being his own boss—he had the time. He ran a company called Concrete Jungle that did high-end interior terrarium-like installations for ultracool offices, stores, salons, and spas, often involving rare ferns, indoor marshes, and, depending on the client, live newts.

"Of course, now her eBay days are over!" came Leo's voice.

She should totally go out with that guy.

"All right. Rock on, Bella. Call me later," said Lola. "If it goes to voice mail, it means Sidecar swallowed my phone."

And boy, would that bum Doug out. He'd proudly scored his wife the prototype of a superfancy Tungsten Bluetooth molded magnesium something something something complete with a contact manager, Web browser, a calendar, e-mail, an MP3 player, a wireless headset, a global positioning system, high-resolution still and video cameras, television channels, interactive restaurant listings, several elaborate games, and the capacity, if you held down the 3, Message, and # keys all at once, to emit a ray that would thwart a missile attack. Or so it seemed.

Lola resented the camera function most of all. "I just need a *telephone*, Doug," she'd said when he insisted she take it. "No pictures. Yes, it's adorable that your photo pops up when you call me. But don't you get it? Generally, I use the phone so I don't *have* to see people." At this moment, Lola briefly considered coating the offending device with Alpo.

"Yep, I'll call you," said Annabel. Lola could hear the squeak of packing tape in the background. "Wait, so when's Daphne coming home?"

"In *six hours and seventeen minutes*," said Lola, finally shaking the dogs off her cuffs. Gibson ran for his metal bowl, Sidecar following, and nosed it along the floor. Not because he was hungry, but because he liked the noise.

Annabel laughed. "Where was she, St. Louis?"

"Yeah," said Lola. "After Atlanta, Miami, Austin, Phoenix, and Chicago."

"Jeez, I thought people said authors don't really do tours anymore," said Annabel.

"Correct. If by people, you mean my ex-publicist," said Lola. Annabel laughed sympathetically.

Quit it, Somerville. Don't let her hear you sweat.

"So you're calculating what, flight in around six, then half an hour in a cab?"

"Yep," said Lola.

The dogs skidded to a stop in the middle of the kitchen floor. "We're bored!" they barked.

"Okay, then. Only like six hours and sixteen minutes to go," said Annabel, switching back to the receiver. "I'll be off in a sec," she said to Leo.

"Take your time!" Lola heard him say.

"How great is Leo?" Lola asked. Earth to Annabel!

"Pretty!" said Annabel. "Look, Lo, I just wanted to say, and I don't know how to do it without sounding patronizing, but I know you may not be a hundred percent happy to hear this kind of thing, about my book and stuff, and I'm just—what can I say? I'm sorry."

"Annabel, it's really fine," said Lola. "But thanks for saying something."

At least she's single.

And I am a total beeyotch.

"Guys! Shhh!" Lola said to the dogs, resorting again to tossing the wombat. She looked at her computer screen.

BE HAPPY FOR HER.

"Annabel, wanna get a drink tonight to celebrate, slash, get our minds off Mimi?" she asked.

Hell's bells. First of all, if she were ever to come through for Quentin, she'd have to get her mind on Mimi the second Daphne came back. And in the middle of her own sentence, Lola also remembered that she'd promised Doug to spend a quiet, romantic evening with him curled up together eating salt-and-peppered popcorn and watching the director's cut DVD of *Evil Dead*.

But you know what? Doug will understand. I have to do this for Annabel. I have to show her how happy I am. And, as always, I have to take this opportunity to prove, especially to Annabel, that I haven't become a married pod person. It's not like I'd be able to stay awake through the whole movie, anyway.

"To celebrate your deal, I mean, not my freedom from bassets," said Lola.

"Well, both. Totally. Call me when Daphne's home," said Annabel. "Thanks, Lo. You rock."

BE HAPPY FOR HER.

Lola hung up the phone and looked at the screen.

Fucking hell.

She opened the fridge, poured herself some of Daphne's Perrier—see, this is why there's only one seltzer guy left—and sat back down, feeling simultaneously listless and vicious. Her eyes wandered around Daphne's computer desktop. Hmm. Wonder what's in *her* Documents folder?

Lola clicked. Now that everyone and her sister and her sister's dry cleaner is writing a book, Daphne must be at work on her second, just like I should be but am not, unless you consider my ceaseless sleuthing-as-research, which is evidently not so ceaseless, as this is really not the kind of sleuthing I'm supposed to be doing.

But I'm just curious. Just a peek. It's not snooping if it's not marked "personal," or "diary."

Lola clicked again.

That's weird.

She looked around again, this time searching the whole computer.

Nope, nothing.

Lola found a ton of Daphne's old etiquette columns—which, she had to admit, were pretty good—but no new book. Not only that, no old book. No drafts, no nothing.

Okay, it's not that weird. Either her first book sprang fully formed from the goddess Daphne's forehead, or all *that* work stuff is on whatever laptop she took with her on tour. Either way, my fantasies about strangling her—just a little!—with that damn pink scarf of hers are really not very sporting.

Or at all appropriate, given last night.

I am going to hell.

Defeated, Lola took the dogs out again. By that point, she was too tired to feel as upset as she really was, which helped. While the dogs gamboled, Lola's thoughts limped along. Okay, if I solve this case—that is, if I ever actually start working on it to begin with—something will break for me, she thought. It has to. Feels like it's all I've got. But jeez, am I going to have to start freaking *blogging* about it?

Back at Daphne's, Lola flopped on the faux-fur couch. She was so tired her vision was blurring; the entire world seemed to have shifted three inches to the left. The dogs clambered up with her, sat down, one on each side, and stared at her with their sad eyes.

There is no way I can have children anytime soon.

"Please, guys, just a little break," Lola begged. "I know! Let's play the sleep game. Whoever falls asleep first wins." The dogs stared. Lola's eyes closed.

What the—? Lola batted at her ear, smacking Sidecar, who'd been busy licking it. Gibson, to her left, was still staring.

Oh. Guess I won.

Wait. Why is it so dark?

Lola hit the indiglo button on her favorite old watch.

It was 9:30 PM.

Sidecar whimpered.

Where on earth was Daphne?

Twelve

Okay. Okay. I just need a moment to thi—

The dogs, sensing Lola's need to concentrate, started to bark.

If I could just get a thought in edgewise.

A faint beep came from Lola's giant bag. Her cell phone, like a kid in a well, was calling for help.

Three messages. Doug, Annabel, and Private Number, in that order, according to the caller ID. Perfect. It's the two people I'm letting down simultaneously, plus ever-fabulous Daphne, no doubt giggling that "something has come up" but she'd be on the next flight from Capri.

The dogs were now sprinting back and forth between Lola and the door, tripping on their ears as they went. Lola toggled between hooking up their leashes and punching into her voice mail, skipping ahead to message three and bracing herself for another day with the dogs.

Nothing. Just a pause, then a click.

Nothing?

Under "received calls," the last incoming number was listed as "unknown." Lola tried the "return this call" option, but the voice mail robo-lady refused. "That service is not available for this number," she said, just to spite Lola.

Nothing. Fine, probably just a wrong number, but then—where was Daphne?

Lola called Daphne's cell. No answer. She left a message.

Then she called Doug. "Sweetie, I'm so sorry, I fell asleep and didn't hear the phone."

"I'm not surprised you conked out," he said. "But where are you now? Wasn't Daphne supposed to—"

"Yeah, that's the thing. I have no idea where she is," said Lola. "And I'm sorry, I know we were supposed to just chill together tonight."

The upside of Daphne's lateness? At this point I don't even have to tell Doug I was going to bail. Nor do I even have to fake-fete Annabel. At least not tonight. In that regard, I am golden.

"It's okay, monkey, it's not your fault," said Doug. "We should have assumed she'd be late, anyway. I think they don't let you take either liquids or solids on planes now, so imagine the security delays."

"I know, but still," said Lola. The dogs, waiting at the door, were emitting low, sad howls. "Uch, I have got to take the dogs out."

"Just take the Doug out sometime, too, okay?"

Ouch.

"Oh jeez, sweetie. I know. I will. I'm sorry," said Lola.

"It's all right," said Doug. "Just saying."

At this point Lola had her hands full with the door and the dogs. "Listen, sweetie, not to change the subject, but can you do me a huge favor and check FlightTracker.com? I've got Daphne's flight info memorized."

Lola had learned about FlightTracker not from Doug but from her mom, who made no secret of the fact that she always used it to make sure Lola's plane had landed safely. "But Mom, I always call you when I land," Lola had said.

"Yes, I know," Mrs. Somerville said, "but the computer is faster than you."

Heading downstairs, Lola heard Doug start tapping on a keyboard. He was never more than a foot or so from some kind of computer, even during *Battlestar Galactica*. "You know, you could do this on that phone I gave you."

"I know, but then I couldn't talk to you at the same time." And then I'd be admitting that the bells and whistles on this gizmo are actually useful.

Tap, tap, tappity tap. The night, a deepening washed-out gray, was warmer than the last. The dogs were quiet now, sniffing vigorously at the trash cans that people had put out for the morning's pickup.

Beep. Call waiting.

"Sweetie, hang on a sec," Lola said. "Bella? I am so sorry. I fell asleep and—"

"Don't worry, I know how wrecked you were. No big." Lola could hear whoops in the background. "Leo came by and we wound up going to Trivia Night at Saloon. You wanna join us? There's this complete hottie on my team who knows even more than I do about French bacteriologists," Annabel said. "He will be mine."

"Annabel, listen. Daphne isn't even back yet!"

"Oh God, you're kidding. She didn't call?"

"Nope," said Lola. "Weird, right? Doug's on the other line checking the flight. I'll call you back."

"Tuberculosis!" yelled Annabel. "Sorry. Jesus. Definitely keep me posted."

Lola juggled the leashes and phone and clicked back to Doug.

"Hi, sweetie, sorry," said Lola.

"Listen, Lo," said Doug. "Daphne's plane got in on time."

"You're kidding."

"Nope. Over three hours ago."

"Okay, there's got to be some explanation," said Lola. "Can you check and see if traffic's bad on the BQE or something?"

"Lo, I can basically hear you, but you're starting to break up. Wanna call me in a few?"

"Sure," said Lola. "Probably 'cause I'm right near the canal bridge." Reception was sketchy there.

"Okay, just be careful over there," Doug said, as far as Lola could make out.

"Don't worry. Anyone messes with me, the dogs will gaze at him mournfully."

"I didn't hear that, but I'm sure it was funny," said Doug.

"Yes, it was. Love you! Bye."

"Lv yw tw," said Doug.

Lola looked around, then at her phone. The signal was weak, but just enough to try Daphne again.

As she dialed, the dogs lurched forward toward the dimly lit Rio Stinko bridge, noses glued to the ground. She quickened her pace behind them. "Whoa, guys, relax," she murmured. "I promise you don't smell a rabbit."

Riiing.

God, that ring sounds really real, like it's—

Coming from that phone lying on the edge of the bridge.

Lola caught up with the dogs and swept the phone up from the concrete. Flashing on the screen were the words "Lola Somerville." The dogs were running in circles, tangling their leashes. As they yanked, something below caught her eye. Before she'd even had time to think, Lola peeked over the railing. All she could make out below was a dark form wedged in some rotted piling. And accessorized with a bright pink scarf.

Thirteen

Lola didn't faint this time. A steely survival calm took over as she yanked the dogs to the other side of the bridge and back into better-signal territory, where she called 911, Doug, and Annabel. Lola squatted down and patted the agitated dogs, speaking softly. "Good dogs. Yes, good dogs. This isn't really happening, so you have nothing to worry about. Good dogs." Touching their velvety ears actually calmed her down, too.

Two squad cars and an ambulance squealed onto the bridge. One cop asked Lola if she'd mind sticking around. She shook her head no. Close behind, someone stopped a rusting beige Volvo— the kind Lola's parents had had back when professors, not lawyers, drove Volvos, which suggested that this one was a family hand-me-down. Wally Seaport got out, notebook in hand.

"That was quick," Lola said to Wally after pointing out the scarf, and what it was attached to, to the police.

"Scanner. Plus I was covering the hunger strike right over at the Organic Depot site," Wally shrugged, with no hint of recognition.

You hoser. We just met—re-met!—and at another murder to boot! What does it take to jog your memory?

Wally tried to follow the cops down the embankment, but one of them stopped him sternly at the already-up yellow police tape. The officer's eyes on them both, Wally settled instead for asking Lola a few perfunctory questions.

No, I don't know anyone who had anything against Daphne.

No, I actually hadn't seen her for weeks.

Yes, that was me with whom you shared two drinks and five shrimp—why, *why*, do they serve romantic tapas in odd numbers?!—a couple years ago at Doomba.

Before Lola could answer that third question anywhere but in her own head, Doug jogged into view. "Excuse me, Wally," said Lola. Doug pulled her into a giant hug, hand on the back of her head, just the way she loved. The dogs, envious, tried to paw their way into the action. Wally went back to the police tape to try to get a closer look.

That was Lola's cue to fall apart. "Sweetie. I. Had. Like. A. *Vision*. Of. This," she cried, her words coming between gasps.

"Whoa. Like, a premonition?"

"No," Lola switched cheeks, her mouth now facing toward Doug on his damp shirtfront. "A fantasy."

"Shhh, baby, shhhh," he said. "It's nothing. Just breathe. Let's sit." He guided her to a curb. They sat. As, for once, did the dogs. Lola breathed.

Before too long, two more headlights swept across their laps. Detective Bobbsey. Bobbsey had a few words with the various people surrounding the body, then trudged back up toward Lola. Dog leashes in one hand, Doug helped Lola to her feet with the other.

"Ms. Somerville," Bobbsey nodded. "This is a first."

"Second, really," she said, trying to wipe away whatever mascara might have raccooned under her eyes. "This is Doug, my husband."

"First, or second?" Bobbsey asked Lola.

"What? Oh, husband?" asked Lola, flustered. "First."

"Sorry," said Bobbsey. "Wife says I should limit the wisecracks."

"Yours, too, huh?" said Doug. Lola, who'd never suggested anything of the sort, knew that Doug, sweet Doug, was just trying to male bond.

That is, before he got protective. "Detective, my wife's not a suspect here, is she?" he asked. "We'd be happy to call our lawyer."

Bobbsey waved him off. "Times of death, types of trauma, buncha stuff I can't tell you—it all adds up to 'don't worry about it.' We could just use her help. Given her apparent gift for body-tracking." He turned to Lola. "The Hoffa people ever call you?"

"No, but I am part basset," Lola said. She told Bobbsey everything she knew, which wasn't much.

"Boyfriend in the picture?"

"You know, I'm not sure. Daphne was a kick. She dated a lot of people."

"Makes sense," nodded Bobbsey, scribbling something down.

"Makes sense?" asked Lola, about to defend Daphne's honor. Daphne wasn't slutty. She was old-fashioned. She *dated*.

Oh, wait.

So Many Men, So Little Taste.

"Wife's beach bag?"

"Yep." Bobbsey nodded. "She and Ms. McKee. They ever date the same person? Quentin Frye. He and Daphne ever an item?"

Man. "Not that I know of," Lola said truthfully, though a competing thought had begun to take shape in her head: one that might give her an edge here, one that she wasn't about to offer up to the detective. Bobbsey wasn't stupid, but the "it's always the boyfriend" theory here was likely the wrong tree to bark up. He knew the victims were both authors, obviously, but perhaps he was naïve about the degree to which commercial fiction could inspire crimes of passion. This *I* know for sure, thought Lola: one person's angry fantasy—my own, say—could be another's vindictive murder.

The flashlight beams down near the water began to skitter closer. Lola and Doug stared; Bobbsey turned. The paramedics were trudging up the small hill with the body in a shapeless brown bag that Daphne really would have hated.

Bobbsey accepted Lola's offer to take in Daphne's dogs for the night; once they'd contacted Daphne's family, he assured her, they'd help make canine custody arrangements. (This service, like the new cut-the-cord command for misbehaving car alarms, was a recent well-received police PR move.)

"By the way, you ever see that guy again? Oddball from the party?" Bobbsey asked.

Reading Guy. "You know, I did, but randomly. At a bodega. Near here, actually. But that was early this morning. Nowhere around here since then. And nowhere near, you know, the bridge. Probably just lives out here," she said, a deliberate shrug in her voice. She was telling the truth, of course, but she also wanted to play her Reading Guy cards close to her vest, just to make that potential angle her own.

Bobbsey didn't write that down. Good.

"Thanks," Lola said.

"You think of anything else, you let me know," said Bobbsey.

Lola and Doug stood and watched his car's taillights shrink to pinpoints.

"Doug, I—" Lola started. "Can't even finish a sentence."

"I know, sweetie, I know. Let's get everyone to bed." He rotated her toward home and urged her forward with the arm he had around her shoulder; with the other, he pulled the dogs along. Lola's left hand held tight, on Doug's waist, to his cotton shirt; her right, in her pocket, to Daphne's cell phone.

Fourteen

Feeling bitterly, dramatically insouciant about germs—we have *other* killers to worry about!—Lola popped out her contacts without washing her hands while Doug ran the dogs out. Too tired to even get under the covers, she flopped on the bed as he came back in. Gibson and Sidecar padded behind, puzzled, but going with it.

"Mimi *and* Daphne," Lola murmured, eyes closed. "Why? Chick lit isn't *that* bad."

"Even if it were," Doug said, curling up next to her and touching her cheek. "I mean, your fatwa on the author of *The Bridges of Madison County* was purely symbolic; everyone knew that."

"Wait a minute," said Lola.

"It wasn't symbolic?"

"Hold on," said Lola, shaking her head.

"The movie was surprisingly touching?"

"No," said Lola. "Wilma Vouch."

"Wilma?" said Doug, rolling back. "As in the Jane Austen Liberation Front?" Lola nodded. The dogs pawed at their legs. "She's strident, irritating, and chooses poor battles, but that doesn't make her a killer," he said.

"I know, but think about it. Can't believe she didn't occur to me hours ago. Two chick lit authors in two days. It can't be a coincidence. Something must have set her off. I mean, who else has that much against them *and* is a little bit crazy?" asked Lola, eyes still closed in thought.

"Well, what about another author? Someone who wants to wipe out the chick lit competition?" said Doug. "Good touch, by the way, being the one to 'find' both bodies."

"Yeah, yeah, I thought of that. But Wilma is even more obvious, I think." Lola opened her eyes and looked at him. "Technically, my book is not chick lit."

"I know, but you know what I mean. Lo, I'm not accusing you! Of writing chick lit, or of committing two murders. I'm just thinking that maybe—"

"Sorry. I know. Reflex. I mean, for God's sake, *Pink Slip* probably would have done better if it had been officially marketed as chick lit. Makes me nuts."

"I know, Lo. Sorry."

"But what *really* makes me nuts," said Lola, "is that so far, it doesn't seem that my book's done well enough for me to make the chick lit killer's hit list."

"I thought you said—"

"Whatever it takes," Lola grinned.

"You are insane." Doug smooshed closer.

"No, you, muffin."

Their lips touched softly, then harder.

Cue bassets. The dogs bounded onto the bed, pawing and snuffling.

Okay, I cannot get work *or* play done with them around, thought Lola. Boy, am I not breeding anytime soon. It's just as well. I am so not ready.

"Lola?" Doug was chuckling, scratching a happy Gibson's nose.

"Yeah?"

He rolled toward her, placed a hand on her belly, and looked her right in the eye.

"Let's start trying."

Fifteen

Trying. "Trying to get more sleep?" Lola asked.

"Yes," said Doug.

No problem.

"Also? To have a baby."

Oh.

Doug kissed Lola again. "I love you, Lo. I want to make more of you. Of us. I've been thinking about it, and I'm pretty sure I'm ready, and I mean that not as a guy who thinks having a Doug Jr. would be 'fun,' forgets the reality of dirty diapers and sleepless nights and having to explain sex and modeling healthy eating habits and figuring out how to be strict about principles and ethics to children without pushing them away. I mean it 'cause . . . I mean it."

I love him.

Shit.

Lola kissed back, long enough to stall, but not long enough to say yes.

"Let's definitely talk about it," she said, eyes closed, lips still near his.

Good. Firm, yet also seductively promising. That oughta hold him.

Doug paused. "Okay, monkey," he said. "I know it's been a long day. A long two days."

"Yeah," said Lola. "In a world that one might think twice about bringing a child into."

Or should I not have said that?

"Well, there's that," said Doug. "We'll talk about it later. Let's get under the covers." Lola rolled over and sank into his spoon, his chin resting on her head. She could normally feel his jaw relax and open slightly as he drifted off. This time, she could have sworn she felt it tense and grind. But she was too sleepy to be sure.

"Lulu, are you all right?"

So much for sleeping past daybreak.

"Yes, Mom, I'm fine. How did—"

"Oh, good. Because I just had this terrible dream where these giant bugs were crawling in your eyes."

Unbelievable.

"Mom, my eyes are fine." Though they could stand to be closed at some point. "But—well, I guess I should tell you. There's been another murder."

"Oh, I know. Isn't it awful?"

"You knew?"

"Saw it on the computer this morning. Poor girl. Her parents must be beside themselves," said Mrs. Somerville. "And I see you found the body again. What are we going to *do* with you?"

Lola was silent for a moment, stunned.

"Mom, has Dad checked the basement for pods?"

"No, why?"

"You just—I thought you'd be more freaked out."

"Well, of course, it's awful, and awfully strange. But I trust you.

You can look out for yourself. And who knows, perhaps you'll be able to help in some way."

"Yeah," said Lola. "Maybe." Well, well. Denial seemed to be working its magic. That, or desperation. Could Mom have read my mind? Have we come to the point where even my mother thinks murder could pad my résumé?

Lola's mind went on a tear. Maybe my parents sense my restlessness, or maybe—chicken? egg?—I'm twitchy because I feel like I'm disappointing them. Have I truly made them happy? Lola wondered, and not for the first time. They're over the moon that I'm married, but, to their credit, they both know that doesn't mean I'm, like, *done*. Far from! Progressive and understanding and artsy, even, as they are, do they secretly wish I had some sort of advanced degree, letters after my name? I'm not exactly struggling for food and shelter, but really, have I accomplished what they'd have liked me to? What do they say about me to their friends? Do they say, "She's perfect!" or do they say, "She's . . . so *creative!*" Have I done enough, been enough? Are they settling, at this point, for a mention or two of me in the tabloids? For the fact that at least I'm around people important enough to be murdered?

Lola's mother's voice cut into her thoughts.

"Just promise me one thing?"

"Sure, Mom."

"I'm sending Dad out to mail you some latex gloves. Please wear them?"

Lola ran the dogs out, gave her plants a cursory watering, felt guilty about that, poured some coffee, peanut-buttered an English muffin, and sat down at her computer. Having guessed that something was off, the dogs were finally quiet. In the scheme of things, Lola actually liked it better when they drove her nuts. Poor pups.

Lola opened *Royalty* in her browser.

Journalists Know Three of Anything Is a "Trend," but Can We at Least Call This a "Pattern"?
Posted by Page Proof

The bruised body of glamorous chick lit writer Daphne Duplex was discovered last night tangled in the pilings along the edge of Brooklyn's notorious Lundy Canal. Ms. Duplex, the author of *So Many Men, So Little Taste*, is the second of two such authors to be murdered in as many days. The body of Mimi McKee, 31, was found stabbed the previous evening at Cabin 9, at the party celebrating the publication of her novel, *Gay Best Friend*.

Burial services for Ms. Duplex will be private, according to a representative for the family.

Police say the smartly dressed victim was strangled with a scarf—her very own trademark pink Hermès—and her body then dumped into the canal, which, despite current efforts at revitalizing, has not lost its reputation as a repository for mob hit victims and other unfortunates.

Police refused to comment on the specific cause of death or to say whether there could be a connection between the two murders. Yet it's not hard to imagine what kind of person might have it in for two such vibrant, successful literary It Girls. For one thing, the popular genre of chick lit has its ferocious detractors, such as the militant Jane Austen Liberation Front, headed by Wilma Vouch.

Hey, that was my theory!
Ugh. Figures I'd be 0.5 step ahead of Wally, for 0.5 of one day. And I call myself a reporter who calls herself a detective.

Police briefly detained the notorious Vouch, whose organization has maintained that this fantastically popular chick lit genre, often featuring flighty singles who can hold down a cocktail better than a man or a job, "demeans women." But does having "no sense of humor" make someone a murderer? Police again declined to say.

Then there's always the age-old motive of envy. Ms. Duplex's body was, coincidentally, discovered by fellow author Lola Somerville,

Spelled right. Thank you.

who was dog-sitting for Ms. Duplex at the time, and who has herself struggled for the kind of recognition enjoyed by many of her peers.

What?

Ms. Somerville is not currently a suspect in the case, according to police. But in the highly competitive world of women's publishing, it would seem only natural that some would want others, well, gone.

Police continue to

Lola sat back in her chair. He did not write that.

She looked back at the screen.

Yes, he did.

Her cell phone rang.

"Where do I start?" asked Annabel.

"Right?" said Lola.

"First, I'm so sorry I didn't call you back last night. The guy at trivia I mentioned, the guy who totally knew about bacillus and stuff? We were making out at The Back Room for like forever, and it's out of cell range, so I didn't know anything 'til I saw the *Day* on my way home. Cover story, natch."

"What was the headline?"

" 'Chick RIP,' " said Annabel.

"Eew," said Lola. "Wait, but what happened to Leo, then?"

"Oh, he dropped me off at home, but then Trivia Guy texted and came to pick me up after."

"Poor Leo."

Shit.

"Whaddaya mean, 'poor Leo'?" Annabel asked, though Lola knew Annabel knew exactly what she meant. Lola meant, "Poor Leo, classic Mr. Right Under Your Nose, bearing and forbearing while you date everyone else."

But she had not meant to *say* that.

Never, ever will I be the married friend who wants her single friend to see the light and settle down.

Or, at least, never will I admit it.

"I mean, poor Leo, missing a good trivia game," said Lola. Wow, *lame*. Change subject. "Annabel, seriously, when do you sleep?"

"From 5 to 5:05 AM. Like you."

"Right," said Lola.

"Anyway. Daphne. The article. What the—*you* found the body?" asked Annabel.

"Pretty much," said Lola. "Grand total of two."

"This is unreal," said Annabel. "PS, Lola, this is not as important as, like, death, but you totally have to call that guy. Wally. I also just read *Royalty*. You have to find out what he has against you."

"You know, I think I wi—"

Lola's cell phone rang. Except she was talking on her cell phone. Plus it was just a beep, not *Mork & Mindy*. Plus her chair had just vibrated.

It was Daphne's phone, still in the pocket of her jacket, which was draped on the back of the chair she was sitting in.

Hell's bells.

How did I forget that I had that?

"Hey Annabel, I—"

I can't tell her I have it. She'd think I'm so blinded by my own ambition that I don't know that keeping the phone is illegal and insane.

But she'd be wrong.

I do know that it's illegal and insane.

"I—you know what?" Lola changed course. "I'm gonna call that dork right now."

Do I answer Daphne's phone?

"It's kind of early," Annabel said.

Shoot, wait, the phone's quiet now. But still. It could be a clue.

"I'm—I'm gonna write out what I'm gonna say, so I'm ready. It'll help clear my head," Lola said. "Call you back."

She fished Daphne's phone out of the pocket.

You dumbass. This is not going to be a clue. Anyone who knows she's dead isn't going to be calling her.

But could someone know I have the phone? Someone besides a basset hound?

Really, very unlikely.

Somerville, remember the difference between sleuthing and snooping.

She looked at the phone. Text Message Received. Read Now?

This is none of my business, thought Lola, pressing Yes.

Sixteen

7:20 AM, citigal: Liam Neeson buying gum @ Hudson
News in La Guardia.

Oh, for God's sake.

Evidently Daphne subscribed—had subscribed—to the same
celebrity-sighting text-messaging group as Lola did. The whole
Celebuphone enterprise was not serious; it was *ironic*, Lola swore.
Though she did wonder why everyone else on the list seemed to
get to spot A-listers like George Clooney or Natalie Portman,
while the only person she ever saw, practically daily it seemed,
was Ethan freaking Hawke.

Anyway.

While I'm here.

She selected Recent Calls.

Lola recognized eight of the ten numbers Daphne had most recently dialed as the access number for Verizon voice mail—she
must have just been checking her messages. The tenth number,
Lola saw, gulping, was her own. That accounts for the mystery call
to Lola's phone, though not for the absence of a message. The

most recent number, though also in area code 718, Lola didn't recognize. She did a quick reverse-lookup on the Internet.

Destiny Car Service, Brooklyn.

The office was only a few blocks away, on Minna Street.

Daphne must have called for a pickup. A gal-about-town like Daphne doesn't wait on taxi lines.

Could one of the drivers have killed her?

Lola did think about that sometimes. Though she'd been in New York for almost a decade, her mom still noodged her about taking cabs at night ("Keep the receipts. I'll pay") instead of the subway, which in Mrs. Somerville's mind still looked exactly as it had in *The Warriors*. But for some reason, Lola's mom—and everyone else—never thought twice about believing that it's reliably "safer" to get into the backseat of a sedan driven by a strange man. Sure enough, you almost never heard about anything untoward, but you have to admit the social contract therein seemed to violate the order of things.

And so did the fact that Daphne had never made it home.

Lola left a note for Doug, threw on her jeans, leashed up the dogs, and set out for Minna Street.

Should she have told Doug where she was going? Probably. But how was she supposed to explain exactly what she was doing? He—like Annabel—would be appalled that she'd taken Daphne's phone and even more appalled that her freelance sleuthing was all part of a bid for glory.

Also, there was that giant elephant in the bedroom wearing a big rhinestone necklace saying, "You kind of left the whole baby thing hanging," so Lola really didn't want to stick around there too long.

Yes, indeed, the note reading, "Walking the dogs, xoxo," should suffice.

Destiny Car Service. Not much wider than its own door, the office was sandwiched between Verrazano's Pork Store and an imposing new cigar bar called Humidor, which pretty much told you everything you needed to know about this neighborhood. The $7 drink and $300 stroller set had moved in (differentiating themselves, still, from the $17 drink and $800 stroller people in Manhattan) but had not yet edged out the superb ricotta cheesecake, Italian funeral homes, and big red-sauce restaurants where you went for lunch after communions.

A couple of Town Cars were parked outside Destiny. Inside were two metal folding chairs, a hardware store calendar with bikini-clad girls holding paint cans, and a giant, yellowed map of Brooklyn with the original neighborhoods—her dad's own Canarsie, for one—that predated the names more recently imposed by colonizing real estate brokers. No North Wayside, no Upper Lundy, no nothing. It was like seeing a map that still said "USSR."

There was an open box of store-bought donuts on the counter—a shame, Lola tsked, in a neighborhood with such good *sfogliatella*. The dogs sniffed the industrial carpet, a smorgasbord of ashes, ground-in dirt, and powdered sugar.

Behind a window of bulletproof glass sat a forty-some-odd-year-old woman with a telephone headset and a giant clip holding back her gray-blond hair. A copy of the *Day* lay by her foam coffee cup, whose top edge was scalloped with salmon lip prints. She was typing furiously, which was impressive, considering the length of her nails.

I can't type that fast, and I bite mine, thought Lola.

"Excuse me," she said.

The woman turned. Her eyes were reddened and bloodshot—no surprise given the amount of cigarette smoke coming from the guys playing dominoes in the back of the office.

"Hi," said Lola. "I actually don't need a car. I just have a question."

The woman waited. She seemed weary. Bet she's heard it all, thought Lola.

"It's about my friend. I think she might have called you for a ride, but she, um, never came home. Do you think someone here might remember the phone call, or anything?"

The woman burst into tears.

"Oh, I—uh, ma'am, I'm sorry, I—"

The woman pushed the *Day* toward Lola like a croupier. She swallowed and sniffed. "Is this your friend?"

Lola paused, then nodded. "Yes."

"Sure, she called us," said the woman, blotting with a Kleenex. "But she never showed up at door four, outside United, like she was supposed to."

Lola took a breath. "Are you sure? You don't think anyone here, anyone here could have . . . ?"

"One of my guys? No way, kid. We're like family. She never showed up, I'm telling you. I called her myself about a thousand times, but she never picked up." A new wave of tears was interrupted by a phone call.

"Excuse me." She pressed a button. "Destiny, where to?"

Lola took that moment to slip Daphne's phone out of her pocket and check Received Calls, which duh, she should have done before. Sure enough. Ten straight calls from Destiny's number.

By then the woman had hung up. "I loved her," she sniffled.

"I . . . Did you know her, too?" asked Lola.

"I was her biggest fan," said the woman.

Oh.

"I loved her book. She was my inspiration," she went on. "See, I'm writing a memoir about my experiences as a single woman running a car service."

Of course you are.

She gestured toward the computer screen, which Lola now saw

was covered with lines of text, not blinking dots on a map or whatever it is a car service would have.

"Wow, that's great," said Lola. "What are you going to call it?"

"Right now I'm thinking: *Destination: Destiny*. What do you think?"

"Not bad!" said Lola. "Two *D*s, that's good . . ." She thought for a sec. "You're a dispatcher, right?"

"Yeah, that plus owner, den mother . . ."

"Right. So how about *Dispatches from Destiny*?"

"Hey, I like it! Thanks."

"You're welcome," said Lola. "Anyway, I'm sorry to bother you. And sorry about, you know."

"Me, too, kid, me, too."

Lola turned to go.

"So what's your name?"

"Destiny."

Ah. Right. "I'll look for your book."

Lola smiled and turned toward the door. So much for that.

Do I want a bakery treat?

Am *I* anyone's inspiration?

As she reached for the door, someone outside did the same.

Oh my God.

Reading Guy.

Seeing Lola, he turned on his heel.

Lola yanked open the door. "Wait!" she yelled.

She tried to run after him, but the loping, distracted bassets held her back. A block and a half away, he got on a bus. The sign said Express to Manhattan. He was gone.

Seventeen

"Uh, hey, Destiny?"

Lola poked her head back in the door of the car service.

Destiny put down her Entenmann's.

"Yeah?"

"You know that guy who was just on his way in here?"

"Yeah?"

"You do?" Lola walked back up to the window.

"Do I know who you're referring to, or do I know who he is?"

"Both," said Lola.

"Yup," said Destiny.

"Who?"

"Can't tell you," said Destiny. "Privacy."

"Are you sure?" asked Lola.

"Yup," said Destiny. She cleared a couple of crumbs from the corners of her mouth with a lacquered thumb and forefinger and turned back to her work.

"Perhaps *this* will change your mind," said Lola, raising an eyebrow and fishing for her wallet.

Damn. Two dollars would change nothing.

Destiny eyed Lola and her crumpled singles. "Nope."

"Okay, thanks anyway!" I am the least cool detective ever.

Lola turned and headed quickly for the door.

Destiny's voice came behind her. "You'll have to wait for the book."

Lola spent her two dollars on an espresso and a copy of the *Day*, to prepare for her irate phone call to Wally. Hello, *New York Day*, it's been a while, she thought. (Doug certainly didn't read it. He actually didn't even read the *Times*; this was mainly a protest against the corny Monday "humor" section he liked to call "Homeless People Say the Darndest Things." Her husband, he got his news from blogs.)

She sat on a bench outside the café. The dogs, still rather listless, settled onto the sidewalk. Poor guys, thought Lola.

Not quite ready to stomach the Daphne story, Lola flipped to the Books section, which at the *Day* was on the limited side, with maybe one story about the increase in TV sports ratings among females after the success of the novel *Football Widow*. Still, a small amount of industry attention was paid to its Chick Lit Bestseller List. Which, Lola had pretended to forget, came out today.

Lola peered at the page.

No way.

Could I possibly be the only one to notice this?

Lola thought for a minute.

She took out her cell and dialed the main number for the *Day*.

Maybe I'm not the least cool detective in the world.

"Wally Seaport, please."

Eighteen

"Seaport."

"Uh, Wally?"

Who else, Somerville? Get a grip.

"Yep."

"Wally, this is Lola Somerville."

"Regarding?"

Jeez.

"We spoke at Daphne Duplex's murder?"

Silence.

"And Mimi McKee's?"

Pause. Lola heard him take a sip of something.

"What can I do for you?"

"Well, for starters, you can tell me why you keep writing bizarre, inaccurate things about me on your blog."

"Miss—I'm sorry, was it Somerville?"

"Yes." And it's Ms., but whatever.

"Two women were murdered in cold blood," said Wally. "I'm not really sure why this is about you."

"Actually, I am," said Lola.

"I'm sorry?"

"C'mon, Wally." She waited.

Lola heard a metallic creak as he leaned back in his chair. He took a deep breath. "How come you never called me back?"

Aha.

"Wally, I—"

"I mean, I thought we had a really nice time."

"We did!"

"So why didn't you call me back?"

"I—look, Wally. I enjoyed meeting you. You're a great guy. But I just wasn't up for taking things any further."

Amazing how easily the *it's over* phrases still assembled themselves. But my God. Am I breaking up with someone I never went out with? Six months after my wedding?

"Fine. Whatever. But that absolves you from returning a phone call?"

"Well, I— You seemed noncommittal about a second date in your message. I figured you were being polite—"

"That makes one of us. And I thought your online advice column—sorry, *former* online advice column—was all about manners," Wally, said.

Ow. Double ow.

"Look, Wally, I'm sorry. I guess I should have called you back. I messed up. I—I'm sorry."

Wally swallowed. "Apology accepted."

"Thanks," said Lola. "Now, here's how you can help me clear my name."

"What?"

"That, or here's how I can tell your boss all about how you bragged that night that you'd actually written that whole 'exclusive from the top-secret undisclosed-location Kabbalah initiation' story from your apartment."

Wally took another sip of something, possibly from a flask in a file drawer.

"What can I do for you?"

Nineteen

At this time of so much death, that an opportunity would present itself to celebrate new life seemed cosmically fitting. Still, Lola had almost forgotten about her friend Oona's baby shower. Good thing Annabel had called her with hungover regret.

But ack, she still needed to buy a gift! So much for her plans to give her poor garden a little love. Doug was heading out to play Ultimate Frisbee. Lola threw on a sundress and kissed him good-bye.

On her way into Manhattan, Lola stopped at the more up-and-came neighborhood nearby, which on a Saturday, with all the sport-utility strollers and darling hats and joyful multi-culti families, was like the Act I finale of *Heather Has Two Mommies: The Musical*. Earlier, she had turned the poor bassets over to an exceedingly charming male cousin of Daphne's—someone who, it had occurred to Lola, might be good for Annabel if by some cruel twist of fate she never saw the Leo light. Now leashless and Snugli-less, in this neighborhood, Lola felt both smugly unencumbered and slightly, sadly, expendable.

At a store called gaga, or googoo, or something equally adorable and lowercase, Lola scored a hypoallergenic cotton elephant woven by the women of a village in Lesotho, spending an extra five dollars to have it gift wrapped in linen because the store didn't "use paper." Except for credit card receipts, thought Lola.

While she was there, she dropped Daphne's cell phone, wiped of fingerprints, into a postage-paid, return-address-free envelope addressed to Wally Seaport.

The timing of the shower is actually excellent, Lola told herself once back on the subway. I'll see everyone cooing and aahing, and I'll get the urge that all those smug ladies who say "You'll see" are talking about. I'll bet I just need to be sprinkled with baby dust or something—and today is my day.

Of course, Lola knew plenty of people with babies, or at least one, or two, on the way. It's just that before she got married—even though she assumed, abstractly, that she would "have kids one day"—it had always seemed like something that would *happen*, not something she'd *do*. Having children, for that matter, seemed like something other people—people with dens—did. Parents were the people who might be described in the *Day* as "the thirty-two-year-old father of four," which always made Lola think that those people were living in some form of dog years, at least two or three for every one of hers. They were not people who, like Lola, still sat with their legs curled up underneath them or wore plastic butterflies in their hair.

Lola also thought of the people she knew who'd had kids and then completely lost their minds. Like those random friends of hers in Chelsea who had tried to prove that they were still cool by having a dinner party when their twins Logan and Caden—one was a girl, but Lola couldn't remember which—were still infants. Lola, brilliantly, suspecting that their apartment was one of those we-take-off-our-shoes-at-the-door apartments, had traded her outfit-making turquoise and green cowboy boots for clogs and de-liberately created a simple, almost bland look that was all about her dangly, multicolored, show-stopping earrings. Which, when she arrived at the door clutching a bottle of sweating Sancerre, she was asked to take off and leave in the designated "guests' earrings" box. "We're doing this for your earlobes," a defeated Lola was told in the foyer. "The twins are real grabbers," said her hostess with a tinkly laugh, "and we don't want to interrupt their experience of curiosity by saying no."

See? Lola thought. I need to solidify my own sense of self before I replicate. Plus, I love being married. But don't I really need to get the hang of *that* before we take it to the next level? *Plus*, I simply can't give my life over to a child till I've reached my "potential" on my own. Otherwise, it—my seminal work, my me-defining next big thing—will never happen. And I'll never be completely satisfied. And—

Hang on, Somerville. Open mind. Remember: just use the baby shower as this-could-be-you research. See how it feels. No harm, no foul. You don't have to get pregnant tomorrow. That's all.

Her gaze wandered around the subway car, whose air-conditioned cool was welcome even though the summer heat hadn't fully hit. Someone facing her was reading the celebu-baby magazine *Bump Weekly*. Lola stared at the cover. "Exclusive photos—IN UTERO!"

On second thought, maybe if I get pregnant I'll get some goddamn ink, she thought, her imagination sprinting ahead. "*Middling Novelist Accepts True Calling. 'I realized that it wasn't my relative, and may I say, undeserved, obscurity that was making me feel unfulfilled,' says Lola Somerville, author of the novel* Pink Slip, *gazing adoringly at her most recent creative project. 'It was just the fact that I hadn't met this little fella.'*"

See, I'm nurturing. Of my career.

Oona's apartment was what Manhattan rental agents called "cozy," or "sweet." She and her husband, Mick, had shared the studio for years: it contained a bedroom and a living room, which were the same. The baby would fit as long as Oona never actually gave birth.

"Hi, Lo!" As it was, Lola could hardly fit her arms around her friend for a hug. Oona, with spiky hair and clunky shoes that weighed more than she did—or used to—was one of those people who didn't "fill out" when they got knocked up, but rather, who seemed to gain only the exact weight of the baby, and only exactly where the baby was. Lola thought she looked pretty hilarious, like the picture in *The Little Prince* of the snake who swallowed the elephant.

As Oona drew her in, she whispered in Lola's ear. "I'm apologizing in advance for my sister-in-law."

"Wha—?"

"Hi! Welcome!" An ash-blond woman in stirrup pants bounded up to Lola. Her knit sweater featured a pattern of beribboned pacifiers. She handed Lola a balloon filled with water.

"Here you go!"

"Thanks," said Lola. "Is this to drink?"

"She's funny!" the woman said to Oona. "I'm Heidi," she said to Lola. "And that's for later," she winked.

"One game, Heidi," hissed Oona. "*One* game."

"I know," Heidi smiled gaily. "I'll let you know when we're ready!" she told Lola. She excuse-me'd her way across the apartment and busied herself with a wayward streamer.

"Can I get you a drink?" Oona asked.

"Can you get *you* a drink?" Lola said.

"I wish."

Huh. Maybe it would be good for me not to drink for nine months, Lola thought.

She sipped her punch, feeling the sweet buzz after a single swallow.

Nah.

"So jeez, Lola, how are you holding up?" asked Oona. "These murders—I mean, so scary!" She patted her belly. "It's like, what kind of world am I bringing Quetzalcoatl into?"

"Quetzalcoatl?"

"Yeah," said Oona. "Feathered serpent god of ancient Mexico."

"Ah. Well. Beats Owen and Milo," said Lola. "I mean, specifically, beats up Owen and Milo at recess."

Oona laughed. "We know it's a boy, but we haven't settled for sure on a name. I just feel like it's too jinxy until he's actually born and living and breathing. I mean, I'm not even really comfortable having a baby shower! But we felt weird just ducking the issue and saying 'he' all the time. So for the meantime, we just picked a name we were sure we'd never ever in a million years actually use."

"Gotcha," said Lola. "Anyway, I'm fine, thanks for asking. Freaked out, obviously, but fine. It's good to be at a happy occasion." She patted her friend's arm just as Oona was swarmed by an arriving group of guests.

Waving and mouthing "Bye," Lola walked over to greet the other guests, vaguely wondering why there was plastic sheeting covering the floor. She was always happy to see Honey Porter, yet another fellow writer. They'd met when Lola had tripped over Honey's laptop cord at Starbucks. Lola was mortified to have been such a klutz, and Honey was mortified to have been caught writing at Starbucks. They bonded.

Honey now had triplets. And she was a single mom. Lola hadn't seen her in forever. Honey had never been spotted commuting between prenatal yogilates and prenatal massage in adorable ensembles from Bun in the Oven. More like Grace Kelly, she had simply vanished for nine months and then reappeared, glowing. Lola imagined this was because Honey was old-school, but realized it was likelier because she'd been too pregnant to move.

"Lola, what a total and complete nightmare!" said Honey. "Mimi, Daphne . . ."

"I know," said Lola. "What say we talk about happier things?" She meant it.

Honey smiled. "No problem, believe me."

"So what's going on?" Lola asked, setting her water balloon carefully on a coaster. "You look amazing, by the way."

She did. As good as ever, in fact. Rested, even. How did she do that? Honey was like a dark, downtown Anna Nicole Smith at the late icon's most pinup fabulous. Her thick ink-black hair was pulled into a French twist; she wore red lipstick and—day or night—black, black, black. Motherhood clearly suited her. While not one for clichés, Honey positively glowed.

"Aw, thanks," said Honey. "Well, the babies are, you know, insane but great."

Lola, forcing herself to do her fieldwork, was listening closely. Both insane *and* great. Hmm. Plus, nice rack.

"Have they started blogging yet?" Lola asked.

Honey laughed.

"Anyway, I'm impressed you're even out," said Lola.

"Well, the neighbors have been a godsend. And the lil' devils still sleep a lot. I think they wear each other out," said Honey. "Also, those mommy movies keep me sane—you know, those morning showings where you can bring your babies? Last week the babies slept through *2 Fast 2 Furious* from beginning to end. It was great."

"Lucky you!" said Lola. "That one always makes me cry."

They laughed. "So are you back working and stuff?" Lola asked. Honey did roughly what Lola did these days: some reported essays, which editors call *think pieces*, and some dumb stuff for money, which Lola called *I don't have to think pieces*. Lola was sure the work question was a safe one, sure to not raise any rivalry; after all, the woman had just had triplets.

"Actually?" said Honey. "My book just came out."

Book? What book? How did I not know about this?

"That's great! Forgive me, I had no idea!" said Lola. "What's it about?" Maybe it's about parenting, or something else I don't care about. I mean, will care about someday soon.

"It's the story of a slightly dizzy but ultimately smart gal who works in the media industry and has to decide which suitor is Mr.

Right—while, all along, learning about life, love, and ultimately, about herself," said Honey.

Lola laughed.

"No, I'm serious," said Honey.

"You're incredible," said Lola. "What's it called?"

"*Eenie Meenie Minie Man*," said Honey. "I'm sure it won't sell. They were going to send me on this big media tour, but you know: triplets. And no husband. So I'll have to rely on the kindness of Amazon reviews. I'll send you a copy. But I promise, you don't have to actually read it."

"Of course I'll read it, Hon," said Lola. "Congratulations." They clinked glasses. "Listen," said Lola, hand on Honey's arm, "Let me go say hi to Sylvie."

"Sure," Honey said. "And I'll go take care of *her*." She nodded toward Blanca Palette, who was sitting on a chair in the corner, glowering as usual.

Sylvie, whom Lola had known vaguely in high school and had re-met through Oona, had just come in. Unlike Honey, she was looking rattled.

Lola had just taken two steps toward her, plastic sheeting crackling, when she was interrupted by three sharp claps from Heidi.

"Okay, everyone, balloons between your legs!" she exclaimed. "Time to play My Water Broke!"

Twenty

After the largest display of good sport-itude in history, in which Lola and all of Oona's friends consented to shuffle around the apartment, water balloons between their thighs, to see who could keep hers there the longest (Honey won), they filled their plates with pasta salad and settled in to watch Oona unwrap gifts. (Apparently Oona had wanted to have a no-gifts shower, but Heidi wouldn't hear of it. Since Heidi's family was in the process of buying a major Manhattan real estate management company, Oona—knowing full well her soul was at stake—had chosen to tiptoe around any risk of alienating her sister-in-law. The one major battle Oona had dared fight—and she won—was her veto of Heidi's other proposed activity: making, and painting, a plaster cast of her pregnant belly.)

Lola swallowed some pesto penne. She looked up at Sylvie, who was leaning on the stove, and patted the three inches next to her on the couch, but Sylvie shook her head. She smiled and cocked her head toward the punch bowl. Lola took this to be the international symbol for "I need to stay close to the drinks."

I'll talk to her as soon as we're done with the gift derby, thought Lola. She turned her attention to Oona and her spoils.

Crib bumpers?

Nipple shields?

Wipes warmers?

Activity Spirals?

My Brest Friend?

Babies *need* all these things?

Lola's elephant, while well received, seemed positively quaint.

"Okay, everyone who's not pregnant, stand in the middle of the room!"

"Heidi?" Oona was smiling one of those not-really-a-smile smiles.

"It's not a game!"

Lola and a handful of other guests allowed themselves be ushered into the corner of the room that was still covered by the plastic sheet.

Please don't tell me there's a bouquet, thought Lola. The whole point of getting married is never having to catch one again.

"Ready?" giggled Heidi, reaching into a bag.

Glittering confetti cascaded over Lola and the others.

"Baby dust!"

Lola picked a sparkle from her tongue and excused herself to go to the bathroom. As she entered and fumbled for the light, a hand reached out from behind the door and closed around her wrist. A voice came from the darkness. "You're going to have to come with me."

Twenty-one

"Sylvie?"

"Lola, I really can't take another minute of this shower. Will you *please* come out and get a drink or something with me?"

Hoo boy. I really need to go home and get something done, not to mention spend time with my husband.

Then again, I so never want to be the kind of person who can't help a friend in need because she has to "spend time with her husband."

"How about Mooney's or Looney's or whatever it's called, around the corner?"

"Anywhere that doesn't attract a pregnant-woman kind of crowd works for me," said Sylvie.

Ah. Say no more.

"Done. Let's go."

As it turned out, the party was ending anyway. Oona's water had just broken for real.

Mooney's/Looney's was a dying breed, but not only because its hard-drinking regulars were slowly killing themselves. More because most downtown "dive" bars had been built three years ago, deliberately trashed by the designer, and then given names like Dive. One had graffiti in its bathroom the night it opened. It was unusual for young women like Lola and Sylvie to come into one of the older joints, especially during the afternoon, but the ancient, pink-faced bartender didn't give them a second glance, likely because he appeared not to move his head very much in the first place.

They carried their pints to a splintery table.

"Lola, it's so gross," Sylvie said. "We've been trying for eleven months now. Meanwhile, it feels like every other couple I know got pregnant from sharing a toothbrush."

Sylvie, an online magazine editor, was one of those people who looks boring but isn't. She never did much with her straight, shoulder-length, dirty blond hair, never wore anything that Lola really noticed or remembered. But that's because, Lola figured, she never felt she had to compensate for anything. Self-possessed and insightful, she basically walked through the world saying, "I'm interesting, so my look doesn't have to be."

Lola laughed. "Oh, God, Sylvie, I'm sorry."

"It's just hard. It's so visceral, this need."

"Of course it is," said Lola. "Otherwise there'd be no babies."

"Uch, and the stupid things people say to me: 'Oh, you're lucky—I *sneeze* and I get pregnant!' or 'Hey, just open a bottle of Bailey's and *relax*.'"

"That's unbelievably offensive," said Lola. *"Bailey's!?"*

Sylvie smiled and rolled her eyes. "Like there's any way to relax when the very first thing you do in the morning is take your temperature and pee on a stick. I swear, my charts look like John Nash's sketchbook. Then boom, what's supposed to be this beautiful mystical life-creating congress is like the Bataan Sex March.

Then all there is to do is wait, so you sit there going nuts and Googling every twinge you feel to see if it could be an early symptom, which is not as crazy as it sounds, because I happened to blow my nose at the ear doctor's the other day and he said that *sniffles* could be a sign of pregnancy."

"Whoa," said Lola.

"Right?!" said Sylvie.

"Yeah," said Lola. "Um. Charts?"

"Wait," said Sylvie. "I'm a jackass. You guys aren't trying right now, are you?"

"Not yet," smiled Lola.

"And after what I've said, you never will, will you?"

"Nope!" said Lola. "Kidding."

Mostly. Lola gulped down some beer.

"I'm sorry I assumed," said Sylvie.

"It's really fine," said Lola.

"I was just so craving finding someone else who can relate. Other than the women on Trying to Conceive Internet message boards who call sex BD for 'baby dance.' "

"Not 'baby dust'?" asked Lola.

"Yeah, well, for that they have special little sparkly emoticons. But get this." Sylvie fished a book out of her bag. It was a bound galley, the prepublication version of a book that gets sent out to reviewers. She handed it to Lola.

Rotten Eggs: Women Who Wait Too Long.

"It's all about how the longer we wait to have kids, distracted by selfish things like having careers or finding someone we'd actually like to reproduce with, the lower our chances of ever getting pregnant sink, and so when our society collapses it'll be our fault."

"I hate people," said Lola.

"Me, too," said Sylvie. "As if we're not freaking *trying* . . . those of us who are, I mean," said Sylvie. She thought for a second. "Remember what it was like to be single?"

"Nope!" said Lola. "Kidding."

"Okay, it's like that, all over again. You feel like the different one, the one that something's wrong with, the kid who's still carrying tampons in her backpack while everyone else is smiling knowingly and beatifically about the special secret they share."

"Babies are the new husbands," said Lola.

"Exactly." Sylvie sighed and smiled. "And remember how when you were single you were weird, but if you were looking you were desperate?"

Lola nodded.

"It's the same. If you don't have a baby you're weird—I mean, I don't mean *you* you are weird, I mean *you*, you know what I mean—but if you're trying you're desperate and panicky and sharing way too much about cervical mucus and liable to steal someone's stroller on the subway."

"Oh, for God's sake," said Lola. "Totally ridiculous."

Am I weird?

Twenty-two

Lola hugged Sylvie good-bye, vowing to hang out with her more often. She turned toward the subway. She had a lot to think about on the way home.

Hey look, it's Leo. Or at least one of his lackeys. Lola had spotted the Concrete Jungle truck—actually, one of those new "green" SUVs, a custom Cadillac Escarole. It was parked outside yet another hip publisher in a converted loft space—Jitney Books, Lola believed it was—between a sleek-looking day spa and a store that, as far as Lola could tell, sold only umbrellas.

I should hang out for a sec to see if Leo shows up, just in case. It's starting to feel summer-sticky already, Lola thought, looking up at a washed-out sky; given that it's the weekend, who knows what trains are running which direction, when. And if anyone will give me a ride home, it's Leo.

And here he comes. It's a rare man who looks good in shorts, thought Lola. He was working a knee-length pair of khakis, yet somehow did not, like so many others, look like little frat boy Fauntleroy. His tailored cotton shirt, spendy leather mandals, and lack of backwards baseball cap definitely helped.

"Hey, Lola!" Leo took off his sunglasses to say hello. "How are you holding up?"

"Hey, Leo. You know. Eh."

"I do know," he said. "Need a lift?"

"After hearing that Honey Porter's got a book coming out, too? Yes," said Lola.

"Damn her!" Leo laughed. "Would my picking you up be just the pick-me-up you need?"

"No way are you going all the way to NoWay."

"Why not?" said Leo. "Just finished a big project—a narcissus pool at that spa, sorta my joke with myself—so I could use a break."

"Are you serious?"

"I'm serious. Hop in."

This guy is awesome. What is Annabel *thinking*?

Lola reached for her phone as Leo cleared some tools off the passenger seat. "I'm just gonna give Annabel a call, tell her about the latest insanity," she said, belting herself in with her free hand. "You can say hi from the driver's seat without taking your eyes off the road."

"Hey, you know what, Lola? Give her like an hour. I just—I know she's still napping."

"Okay," said Lola, shrugging. Well, that's awful sweet. As she slipped her phone away, something in the passenger side mirror caught her eye. She whirled in her seat, the belt instantly reddening her neck.

Reading Guy had just finished scribbling something—Leo's license number? A goddamn book idea?—on a small pad. He stuffed it into a pocket, turned on his heel, and ran down a nearby staircase to the subway.

What on earth?

"Sorry! Hang on," Lola barked. She was out the door, down the stairs, and through the turnstile in moments, swiping her MetroCard as she flew. The moment she reached the subway platform, the train doors closed. The station was deserted.

Being followed just cost me two bucks, thought Lola.

Being followed?

Should I really flatter myself?

Could it indeed be that my book *has* been successful enough to merit my violent death?

In broad daylight?

Right. Get over yourself, Lola Somerville.

Lola headed back through the turnstile, only then noticing the hand-markered sign reading: "Every other J train running on the G line, unless alternate side parking suspended." In New York subway language, this message translated roughly as, "You'll be two hours late," or, *"Mmwwwahahah!"*

Huh. At least Reading Guy will never, ever get where he needs to go. Lola suppressed yet another smile. Come on, Somerville, this is serious business. Four sightings is no coincidence; four sightings interspersed with two murders is no joke. But still: what on earth could Reading Guy want with me? I *honestly* don't think he is trying to kill me, thought Lola.

She paused on the stairs, gripping the grimy handrail.

Yet.

Twenty-three

Lola's phone rang as soon as she got aboveground. "Annabel! How ya feeling?"

"Better than that time in Peru with the giardia, thanks," said Annabel. "But listen, Lo, I need your help."

"Bella, you make better cheese grits than I do at this point." Their preferred hangover helper.

"No, it's not about grits—"

"Paella?" Lola reached Leo's van, the door still open as she'd left it. Of course he'd waited. "Sorry about that," she told him. "Annabel," she added, pointing to the phone. She explained to Annabel where she was.

"Oh, awesome, so you are still in Manhattan. I just realized I— I kinda need . . ." Lola didn't think she'd ever heard Annabel sound so tentative. ". . . I need to ask you a giant favor."

Finally, thought Lola. *Finally.* She turned toward the street and whispered, "You want me to take the subway so you and Leo can, like, *hang out?*"

Annabel paused.

Uh oh.

"Noooo," said Annabel.

Goddammit, Somerville.

"See, in all the excitement I totally forgot that Poncho needs to see a proposal," Annabel said. "For the book. The deal's as good as done, but they want something in writing from me anyway."

Lola knew the drill. It's just that for her, the something in writing came *before* the done deal. And the done deal didn't always come after the something in writing.

"And they need it tomorrow."

"Tomorrow?" said Lola.

"Yeah," said Annabel. "By lunchtime. They're taking me to Qwerty."

"Qwerty!" The beyond-hot downtown publishing hangout that felt like it should be uptown (the likes of which, in fact, had driven many of its neighborhood's residents to Brooklyn, where they clung to their last shred of hope of keeping it real). "And you need my help deciding whether it's morally acceptable to order a $110 hamburger?" Lola asked.

Qwerty's signature dish was a Kobe-beef burger filled with foie gras, black truffles, and Beluga caviar, served with bald-eagle egg aioli and a sprinkling of gold dust.

Qwerty. Jesus.

"Well—" said Annabel.

"Yes," said Lola. "Yes, it is. If you save me some fries." Crisped in lobster oil, this Lola knew.

I cannot believe she gets to go to Qwerty.

"Actually, Lo, it's the proposal. I've never done such a thing. I don't know where to start," said Annabel. "Other than calling you. I know my timing sucks ass—but I was wondering if you could just sit with me for an hour or two and help me get started?"

I cannot believe she gets to go to Qwerty with my *Cyranoed proposal.*

"Hey, Leo?" said Lola. "Thank you so much for waiting, but it looks like I'm not gonna need that ride after all."

Twenty-four

Lola walked toward Laptop, the West Village bar known for welcoming writers who camped out all day with their "novels." (Though since it also offered wireless access, Lola suspected most used the time to e-mail their parents to ask for money.) She'd declined Leo's offer of a ride uptown in order to give herself a brief chance to think—and to rally herself into a helping mood.

I have to, *have to* do this for Annabel, thought Lola, even though I was really hoping not to have to think about her book deal until I landed mine. I *cannot* be the married best friend who blows her off out of petty competition and jealousy just to go home and hang out with my husband. I just can't.

And bottom line: she's Annabel. She'd do it for me.

"Hey wait, where'd you get the laptop?" Lola asked, scooting a chair up to the zinc table. Annabel had done most of her blogging from a Mac at a Kinko's. Free. The manager was also a bass player; they'd had a thing.

"Leo," Annabel said. "Loaner. He's got like a ton of them."

"Tell me about it," said Lola. "Our place looks like the Apple Store."

Something flickered across Annabel's face. "Leo's place," she said, "looks like Johnny Appleseed's."

Lola inwardly smacked herself. Right. I always forget. Annabel and Leo are not an "our place" couple. Totally misplaced bond-over-boyfriends moment.

"To the hair of the dog," she said, raising her glass, hoping Annabel would let it go, and wondering just how much beer she was going to drink that day. Clink. "And, Bella," she smiled extra-wide, "to your good fortune."

"You mean the best friend who's totally bailing me out?" Annabel smiled.

Am I just paranoid, Lola wondered, or was that a little forced?

They hunkered down for a while, brainstorming the intro and the marketing suggestions and a list of chapters, pausing only for Annabel to hop up for another round of Bowery pilsner. Lola tapped in a few changes to what they'd written. Wow, she thought, I really do know what I'm doing. That, actually, is a little reassuring.

Annabel came back with the beer.

How did she manage to look so hot in overalls?

"Love that!" Annabel said, putting down the glasses. "On the house!"

"How come?" asked Lola, pretty much knowing the answer. Annabel shrugged. "Just 'cause," she said. She gave the bartender an almost imperceptible smile. Lola thanked every god she could think of that her single days as the "cute friend" were over.

Lola's phone rang. Then so did Annabel's.

"Hey, sweetie," said Lola. "Doug," she mouthed to Annabel, raising her "gimme a sec" finger.

"Hey, dude," said Annabel. "Leo," she mouthed to Lola.

Lola gave Annabel a knowing, approving glance. How cute! Both their boys—*dammit!* Again she'd forgotten that Leo was only her imaginary boyfriend. Annabel's imaginary boyfriend. In *Lola's* imagination.

She told Doug when she thought she'd be home. "Bye, swee'-pea."

Annabel was already off the phone with Leo. "You guys are so cute and happy, just in that everyday, lives-woven-together kind of way," she said.

No, no, no we're not! Lola wanted to say. I mean, we are, but you know. No flaunting. Please don't let her think I got all cute and happy right in her face.

"I mean, when Leo 'calls to check in,' it's a little needy," Annabel went on, looking right at Lola. "When Doug does, it's sweet. Am I right?"

"All I know about being married," said Lola, dodging, "is that I'll never have to hear 'Your life is *so Sex and the City!*' again."

"I hear you," said Annabel. "Though I honestly never tire of 'Your life is *so Oz!*'"

One more beer later, they got to a stopping point on the proposal. "I'm good with the rest," said Annabel. "I wasn't sure you'd— Lola, thank you so much. Really."

"Bella, of course," said Lola, a little woozy, glad she'd had seconds of the penne. "E-mail it to me when you're *done* done if you want Doug to print it out all fancy."

Lola hugged Annabel good-bye. You know, she thought, that didn't suck as much as I thought it would. Always nice to be needed, I guess.

Now to remind my poor husband how that feels.

Twenty-five

Lola dropped her keys in the dish by the door.

"Sweetie?"

"Sweetie, it's me."

"Lola."

No response.

"Lola Somerville? From the wedding?"

There was music coming from the kitchen, something Lola was pretty sure she recognized as the soundtrack from *The Day the Earth Stood Still*, which was something Lola was pretty sure she'd never recognize if she weren't married to Douglas B. Garfield.

Her husband was just setting down a screwdriver as she walked in, slipping her bag from her shoulder.

"Hi, Pumpkin Pie," he said, enveloping her in a hug. She loved it when he called her that.

"*Klaatu barada nikto.*" One good turn deserves another. She wasn't sure exactly what it meant, but it had stopped a robot from destroying the world.

"Ooh, say it again," he murmured.

"*Klaatu*—wait." Something behind Doug had caught her eye. "Is that a computer?" Lola asked.

Doug stepped aside proudly. "I thought it would be good to have one in the kitchen. You know, like a virtual cookbook, plus, see, they're all networked together so we can play music from any hard drive, and—"

Lola pulled him back toward her. "I love you."

It felt like they hadn't had sex in a while. It felt good. And Lola was only too happy to reconnect with her husband without having to actually discuss anything, even just the fact that they'd hardly even hung out lately.

"You know, Lo?" Doug wound a tendril of her hair around his finger. The sheets lay in a tangled zigzag across their bodies.

"Mmm?"

"We've hardly even hung out lately."

Crap.

"Well, what with the double murder and all," she said. "I've been so preoccupied. Quentin, you know. He's a little needy . . ." She was willing to hint that she was still helping Quentin but thought it was perhaps not time to tell Doug that "helping" might mean a bit more than offering hard-drive maintenance and moral support.

"There's that," Doug replied. "But even so. Even before that—"

"There's also been a lot of stuff going on with friends," said Lola. And she was proud of herself for not letting those things slide. "Oona's shower—"

"Of course. But you're not, like, avoiding talking about the baby thing, right? Did I completely freak you out? I mean, by definition, it's the kind of thing we should work through together."

"No, sweetie, no," Lola lied. It's less of a lie if you lie about feelings, right, and not facts? "I mean, yes, it is that kind of thing, but no, you didn't. Freak me out. I just . . . haven't had time to think. And that's what I need. Time to think." Time to think about how I feel like I'm letting you down. Time to think of more ways to avoid saying, "I don't know if I'm ready, at least not until I know if I have this book deal." Gah.

Doug paused. "Okay." He thought for a sec. "Hey, Lo. I got an idea. I know you're behind on work and stuff. But can you play hooky tomorrow?"

Shit. No.

"Sure," she said.

"Let's get away from it all," he said. "And not talk about anything important, or even interesting."

"And not eat anything at all healthy?" she asked.

"Right. MozzArepas and raw clams of death."

She knew it. "Coney?" Their favorite island getaway.

"Coney." Coney Island, indeed.

Actually, Lola? Let's think for a second. On this murder thing, I'm working my own angles, and right now, one of those angles should be working all by itself. So: Coney, quality time with husband, frozen chocolate-covered bananas—

"Done," she said. "See you on the Cyclone."

"See you sucking at Skee-Ball."

Lola threw a pretend punch, which her husband deftly blocked with a few patented moves of Doug-fu. Lola cracked up. But before she could register that Doug was looking at her in that "let's not get out of bed yet" kind of way, she remembered something exceedingly important.

"Hey, what time is it?" Lola looked at her watch.

Ha. If all had gone according to plan, her insanely far-fetched but still worth a try plan, the online version of what she was waiting for should be up now.

"Oh! C'mere," she said.

Lola leapt out of bed, threw on Doug's sweatshirt, and trotted into her office, then right back out. "No, no, I'm gonna try the schmancy new kitchen computer!"

Doug padded up behind her wearing only glasses and boxers. It was a good look, Lola noticed in passing. "What are you doing, crazy lady?" There was a glint of weariness in his voice, but Lola ignored it. He'd see.

She clicked around for a minute, then smacked the countertop. "Yes!"

Twenty-six

Pink Slip
Lola Somerville's Debut Novel Makes You Glad She Lost Her Job
By Ida Julep

"Oh, my God," said Lola.

"Wait, is that you?" asked Doug, leaning in to see.

"No, it's the other Lola Somerville with a debut novel called *Pink Slip*," said Lola. "But I'm cuter."

"But how—?"

"Just read."

You may remember Lola Somerville as the plucky columnist who exposed—live on an episode of *Penelope!*—the conspiracy behind the once-cool, now bankrupt Ovum network. That, ladies and gentlemen, was some good television. But if you don't remember her from that, you should remember her from her new novel: the fanciful, fictionalized account of how that particular dot-com went bust. And this, ladies and gentlemen, is some good reading.

"Holy Hannah," said Lola.

(Those gentlemen, that is, who read chick lit—and we love you, whoever you are.)

"Oh, for God's sake! Why is everything written by a woman, about a woman, considered chick lit?" said Doug. "And everything by a man about a man is just lit? Unless it's lad lit, but that was over before it began."

"Hey, that's my speech," said Lola.

"Hey, you're my wife," said Doug.

By turns hilarious and heartbreaking, Somerville's novel perfectly captures the heady days of the online gold rush and fin de siècle search for meaning, gleefully skewering its opportunistic taskmasters and our own earnest credulity. Still, at its heart, *Pink Slip* is a timeless tale of love, friendship, family, and ultimate faith in oneself. Don't read it if you don't want to laugh out loud on the subway—or if you can't afford to get so absorbed you miss your stop!

"Of course, it was also a major exposé, but whatever! I'll take it!" cried Lola.

Doug whistled. "I guess so! But how—why now? I guess what I mean is, what took them so effing long?"

Lola shrugged. "It's the *Day*, Doug. They're lame."

"Whatever. I'm really proud of you, monkey." He gave her a massive trademark Doug hug. "You deserve it."

Well, yes and no.

"Wally, thank you for the review," said Lola.

"No problem." He sighed. "I actually—well, way back when the publisher's galley had arrived in the office, I'd seen it on Ida's desk, and I—I took it. I—well, if you really want to know, I wanted to see if I was in it."

"Oh, I—well, it wasn't about—I mean, you wouldn't—"

"No, I know, it's cool. I actually wound up thinking it was awesome."

"Oh, thanks!"

"Which is why I, embittered, didn't give it back to Ida."

"Oh," said Lola. "Gotcha."

"Until now."

"Right."

"So."

"Look, I'll let you go, Wally. But really, thanks. You've outdone yourself."

"I try."

"Who-hoo!" It was Annabel.

"Right?" said Lola. "It'll be in the print version tomorrow."

"So that's when the movie agents will call, et cetera, et cetera?"

"Yes. I shall wait by the phone. Because we all know how well that works. Actually, for you it seems to be effective." Lola hoped her tone sounded light enough. "Are you all set with the proposal?"

"Yep. Just in time for me to head out with Ismail the Albanian model."

"You amaze me, Bella," Lola said sincerely. "Are you sure you don't want to—" She stopped herself. "Did you ever know that you're my hero?"

"I do what I can," said Annabel. "Hey, so what's happening with the mystery, Brenda Starr? Any suspects yet?" Lola had hinted to Annabel, a little more strongly than she had to Doug—Annabel was far less of a worrier—that she was sort of kind of "working the case."

"Not yet," said Lola. "But assuming someone—or something—cooperates, we're about to get a big break."

"You wanna vague that up for me a little?"

Lola hemmed. "Well, I—I think for now it's best if I don't tell you—"

"Seriously?" asked Annabel.

". . . Yeah," said Lola.

"Not even a little?"

"I—"

"Lo, what could possibly be so off-limits? Remember me? Annabel? From the telling each other everything?" Annabel's tone was light, but she was right; this was a first.

"I know. Of course. I'm sorry. It's just—it's delicate. I . . . need to do this myself. For me," said Lola.

This sucks.

Annabel sighed. "Okay, Lo. I'll just take that as the New Age way of saying you could tell me, but you'd have to kill me."

Or, *you'd* have to kill *me.*

Twenty-seven

"I'm thinking we better enjoy this place while it lasts," said Doug. He and Lola had ridden the F train to its last stop, aboveground, fondly watching the Coney Island skyline come into view—the stubby "space needle," the rickety roller coaster, the red-girdered parachute jump ("Brooklyn's Eiffel Tower!")—all set into relief against a blue-gray ocean and matching sky. Coney's shabbiness, its seediness, was exactly what held wonder for them. So unglamorous it was fabulous, Coney Island was basically Six Flags' little burnout brother. A bit sinister, too: the bars were scarred by shootouts, the boardwalk haunted by souls lost to the brothels. And yet Coney's wanly twinkling lights also held glimmers of its faded glory, the days when a carousel was all it took to enchant a child, and before that, when the amusement park's 250,000 electric bulbs were themselves the attraction, like a star whose beams, eons old, have just landed on earth.

But all that was about to change. A mustache-twirling developer had purchased massive swaths of land, from the projects to the shore, and had announced plans for a "Vegas-style" "entertainment destination" including an indoor ski slope, a wild game hunting range, a "swim with dolphins" pool, the "world's tallest mall," a re-creation of the entire French Quarter of New Orleans, and transport from Manhattan by blimp.

"Seriously," said Lola. "When the digging starts, let's lash ourselves to a tree. Or," she added, looking around in vain for a tree, "a funnel cake."

Doug agreed. "Freak show?" he asked.

"Freak show," said Lola.

For some couples, romance means a carriage ride in Central Park. For others, Tavern on the Green. Or Venice. For Lola and Doug, romance was the famed Coney Island "freak show," a rare vestige of Barnum-esque sideshows—only without the pitiful displays of "human oddities." *These* human oddities were, shall we say, skillful? Fire eater, sword swallower, escape artist, the guy who hammers the screwdriver into his nose: Lola and Doug loved it all. For them, it wasn't about being grossed out; it was the simple low-rent honesty—yes, honesty—of the whole enterprise. No smoke, no mirrors, just a guy eating a lightbulb.

So, hand in hand, past the teeny old candy shop shuddering under the weight of the soon-to-expand subway station, past the screaming neon "Bump Your Ass Off " invitation to ride the bumper cars, past the guy selling balloons on sticks and piña coladas in plastic cups, past the teeny taqueria with the Magic Marker menu, to the freak show they went. They waved at the barker outside, who was flanked by the Tattooed Man and an alterna-Vanna wearing a live yellow python like a stole. Passing the dented four-seat bar, Lola's favorite bar in all of New York, which served only Genessee Cream Ale and Zima, they entered the dingy "theater" and, squeezing past a family of alarmed tourists, took their seats. The splintered bleachers climbed to a low ceiling; naked lightbulbs—those not yet eaten—dangled from wires wrapped around exposed pipes. On the scuffed black stage, a dreadlocked woman, tattooed head to toe and her lip pierced clear across like the spine of a spiral notebook, had just slurped up a live worm. A recent addition to the cast, her name was Insectivora. Lola was in heaven.

Insectivora plucked a wriggling cockroach out of a plastic box and licked her lips. The audience gulped, peeking at her from between split fingers. Suddenly, the roach escaped her grasp and fell to the stage, on its back, legs waving. Insectivora shrugged and scooped it up, bringing it hungrily toward her mouth.

"I can't believe she's going to eat that right off the floor!" Lola exclaimed. Everyone laughed.

"You put the LOL in Lola." Doug grinned.

Then came the redheaded Electra, whom Lola recognized from outside, even without the python. Electra sat gamely on a scary-looking chair wrapped in wires and bulbs like vines on Lola's trellises. After a giant switch was thrown—sending "thousands of volts surging through her body!"—a fluorescent bulb lit up at the touch of her hand!

"Yeah!" yelled Doug, clapping furiously, though he'd seen the act a thousand times and knew perfectly well, and in fact would happily inform you if you asked him, that the secret was a hidden transformer that, though high in voltage, was harmlessly low in amperage, and so, when Electra touched a metal plate on the chair, she received the current without feeling it and thus was able to light the bulb, which was not of the common incandescent variety, but rather a special type of bulb designed precisely for such a high-frequency current.

Lola felt a swell in her heart. She and Doug were just here, just now. Nothing else mattered.

Except the fact that Reading Guy had just walked in.

Twenty-eight

"DougI'mreallysorryI'llberightback," Lola whispered.

"Whuh?" he said.

But she was gone.

Leaping down to the doorway, Lola looked around. No sign. A guy at the bar with a bull ring in his nose raised a glass. No one else in sight.

She raced out to the street. Still no Reading Guy. Just families, clots of idle teens, and a woman in a sequined smoking jacket on stilts.

I was sure that was him, she thought. Positive.

Really, totally sure.

Completely.

Right?

She leaned against a wall.

Let's say it was. Is it fair to say he's following me now? Is it fair to say I only *thought* I wasn't thinking about this today?

Doug came around the corner.

"Hey," Lola said. "You didn't have to leave! I told you I'd be right back."

"I know, but the Human Pincushion just isn't the same without you," Doug said. "So what's going on? I figured you were going to the bathroom, but then I saw you run for the door instead, and anyway, you don't throw up *before* you eat the clams."

"I just . . . okay." Lola took a breath. "Can we get a Genessee?"

They clinked paper cups. "Okay," said Lola, popping her hair into a scrunchie and hooking the heels of her clogs on a barstool rung. "Remember that guy from the Mimi night? Reading Guy?"

"Yeah," said Doug.

"I thought I saw him."

"Okay," said Doug. "So?"

"And I feel like he could be involved somehow with the Mimi thing. Or even the Mimi and Daphne thing."

"Uh-huh . . ."

"And see, remember how Quentin asked me to help him out?"

"Yeah, with those files?"

"Mmhmm, but there's more. He actually wants me to help find the killer."

"Help find the killer? Why—"

"Because he thought I might be good at it?"

"No, duh. I mean, why didn't you tell me? I could help you! That's what we do best together, besides making tempura."

"I . . . I thought you'd think I was crazy."

"I do think you're crazy, monkey." He kissed her. "So should we go look for this guy, or what?"

"Oh, no, I—" Lola took a gulp of ale.

I can't tell him why I need to do this myself, she thought. *I* need the kudos. I need to not be a "husband and wife team," other than in real life. I haven't proven myself on my own yet; I need to do that first.

"I . . . Nah," said Lola. "I'm sure that wasn't him. Anyway, I'm keeping this 'detective work' to a desk job, pretty much—you know, Willow-from-Buffy stuff—thanks to all the hacking skills I learned from my husband."

Doug smiled, proud of his wife. "Lemme know if you run into a particularly thick firewall."

"Totally," said Lola. "But you know what? Susan Thunder is off today." The most famous female hacker. Doug kissed Lola in appreciative delight. "Hey, let's ride the Cyclone!" she said.

Coney Island's famed roller coaster was another monument in Doug and Lola history. It was, in fact, where Doug had proposed.

"Done," said Doug. "Monkey, I'm so glad you told me what's been going on with you. I mean besides the obvious insane freak-out over Mimi and Daphne, and also besides maybe the baby thing that we're totally not talking about so forget I said it. Seriously. I could tell that something else was bugging you—I mean, that's what happens when we don't tell each other stuff. Okay? Okay. Oh, and you can finish—"

Lola had just polished off Doug's Genessee.

"—my ale."

They boarded the Cyclone. As they buckled in and waited for the other cars to fill up, Lola felt the ale, inhaled on an empty stomach, start to fizz toward her brain. No, wait. It wasn't going to make it all the way to her brain; it was stopping at her mouth.

"Doug?"

"Yeah, monkey? What, I forgot to 'remove all wigs'?" A little giddy, he pointed to the painted sign that cracked him up every time. Which reminded him: he removed his glasses and stuck them in a case in his pocket.

"No, I—" Lola started. Just then, the ride did, too. A cheer went up. Clack clack clack, up the first steep hill. Lola had to raise her voice. "I—I think I want to do this by myself."

"The roller coaster?"

"No, the—" *Whooosh!* They zoomed down the first hill. "—the helping Quentin."

"Okay . . ." said Doug. "Why?"

"Well, because . . ." And suddenly Lola was talking. Talking and talking. Everyone else was screaming and whooping, but she was talking. Out came all her bitterness and frustrations from the past couple of years, her disappointment about her book, her resentment of her more successful peers, all of it. The Cyclone went up, down, around, and up, down, and around again, and, over all the noise, over all the lurching and whooshing, Lola talked.

As they coasted to the end, Lola wound around to her conclusion. ". . . So I just really feel, I just really feel like *I* need to get the credit. Myself. And then write a book."

Doug nodded. He helped her out of the seat, and then looked at her.

"I understand," he said. "But just so you know? While we were up there, I was going to re-propose."

Twenty-nine

For the first time in fifteen minutes, Lola was silent.

She slumped back into the roller coaster seat, only to be glared at by forty teenagers waiting their turn. Doug reached out a hand to help her up again, cocking his head toward the exit. They went out to the street and stopped by a cotton candy and chimichanga stand.

"Look, I get it. I know you. All that stuff was on your mind. Majorly, obviously. It had to come out when it had to come out," said Doug. "I'm just glad that wasn't my first attempt at proposing."

Oh good, thought Lola, I'm pretty sure he just smiled. Jesus, I suck. "How about a do-over?" she asked, gesturing weakly at the coaster.

"Hmmm, no," Doug said. Ow. "I'll wait for the next 'the time is right' time."

"Doug," Lola said, "I'm really sorry. I just—I'm *really* sorry. I know I've been hard to reach. And my self-absorption just reached new heights."

"Eighty-five feet, to be exact," said Doug, looking back at the Cyclone.

Oh, God.

He grinned. "I kid!" Serious again. "It's eighty-nine feet."

"Dammit, Doug!" Lola laughed. Oh, thank God. Okay. This feels better already. "Sweetie, please do not ever mistake my self-involvement for lack of love." Lola wrapped her arms around Doug's waist. "I adore and appreciate you every minute of every day. And I swear I will not let my self-absorption reach Cedar Point Top Thrill Dragster heights."

"Mmmm, the tallest . . . 420 feet, ninety-degree incline, speeds up to 120 miles per hour," Doug murmured. "How did you know about that ride?"

"I'm married to *you*," said Lola, kissing him.

The next few days passed mercifully murder-free, just as Lola had hoped. She spent the time hunkering down with her Mac, finishing up an assignment for *Stylicious* called "Is It Time to Break Up with Your Friend?" that was remarkably, though not actionably, similar to stories she'd written the year before, and the year before that, which were entitled, respectively, "Spring Clean Your Social Life: Do All Your Friends Still Fit?" and, yes, "Is It Time to Break Up with Your Friend?" After finally doing some emergency gardening—stripping some dead leaves from her peonies and giving her honeysuckle a haircut—she wrapped up a reported essay for Frisson.com about the social history of female action figures. This stuff, she loved. And Doug was happy to lend his *Tomart's Price Guide to Action Figure Collectibles* to the cause.

"I can't decide if it would be cool or uncool if they made an action figure of you," said Doug, having corrected a few of her facts. ("No, Lady Jaye didn't have swivel-arm battle grip. Baroness did.")

"Um, cool?" said Lola.

"Right, but would it also be, like, objectifying?" He thought for a second, eyes on the ceiling. "No, yeah, it would be cool."

Doug put the book back down and massaged the back of Lola's

neck. "Hey, haven't you written articles about how married couples should have, like, Date Night?"

"Yes," said Lola. "I believe that tip appeared in my articles '10 Ways to Make Your Marriage Sexier,' '15 Ways to Get That Spark Back . . . Tonight!' and '20 Ways to Make Your Marriage Sexier.'"

"I trust you got paid double for the twenty?" laughed Doug. "No, really. How about tomorrow? Let me make you dinner. It'll be our do-over from Coney."

Oh dear. Tomorrow could be bad.

He was nuzzling her neck. "I'll fire up the kitchen torch." That could mean only one thing: crème brûlée.

"Mmmmmm," said Lola. "Sweetie, I would love that." She nuzzled him back. "But can it be Saturday?"

Doug leaned back. "Saturday. Well, I'm supposed to volunteer at Tekserve, which I'd rather not miss. But I guess if we had to . . . Why, what's tomorrow?"

"Well, I'm not sure yet. But it could be something good and fun, and I'd want you to be with me," said Lola. "Thing is, there's a chance it might not happen, so—"

"Jeez, Lo, what is it?"

"You'll see. Or not. Uch, sorry. I promise we'll have our dinner, sweetie." About her ongoing machinations—which were much more, of course, than the "desk job" Lola had described—Lola just couldn't bring herself to admit the details to Doug. Not just because they were, potentially, crème brûlée for her ego, but also because they could put her in danger.

I want him neither to stop me nor to think I've sunk this far.

"Okay, Lo, whatever," said Doug. "You know what, better let's wait for a night we can definitely commit to. And maybe until your basil is just a few days bigger."

"That works," Lola smiled as sweetly as she could. She pulled her husband close. Let's just get through the next couple of days, she thought, and then I can go back to avoiding the discussion about children.

Lola got up early, even for her, and opened the *New York Day*'s website before even checking her garden. She paused briefly to ac-knowledge the generally brilliant front page headline (naked guy stranded on midtown windowsill: "Moon Over Manhattan"), then clicked to the Books page.

Yep.

There it was.

I cannot freaking believe this worked.

Thirty

Lola had rallied Doug and Annabel to meet her at Earl's, a steakhouse in Manhattan's meatpacking district that dated back to the era when denizens of the district actually packed meat. The crooked cobblestone streets, once awash in blood and feathers, were now lined with velvet ropes and limos. Basically, it made SoHo look like New Jersey's Paramus Mall.

Earl's, on the other hand, at the farthest edge of the district at the West Side Highway, was like the lone building standing after a pashmina hurricane. Old wooden bar, career waiters in white, giant thick steaks, creamed spinach. Writers hung out there, real writers, escaping their better-known haunts now overrun by college kids in the Village and the tourists in midtown. Lola thought of it as the Algonquin: West.

Lola also happened to know that Earl's massive, dungeonlike basement contained a meat locker, as any self-respecting scary basement must.

Lola and Doug ordered gin and tonics, their house drink in the summer, unless Doug was in the mood to muddle mint for mojitos.

The bartender slid the tumblers toward them. "Oh, and um, I'm Lola Somerville?" Lola told the bartender.

"Oh! Hang on!" He peeked down at something behind the bar. "Cool. On the house! Yours, too, buddy. Why not?"

Lola grinned.

"Wow, thanks. What—?" Doug asked, fishing out a couple of singles.

"Tell you as soon as Annabel gets here," Lola smiled.

Beep.

Lola's phone announced a text message. She hesitated, sensing that she should be giving Doug her full attention.

Okay, just a quick peek.

9:04 PM, krispykremey: Honey Porter at Bergdorf's, highlighting her highlights

Beep. Another.

9:05 PM, snowwhite: Who the hell is Honey Porter?

Hooo-kay, Lola thought, we'll leave out that part when I tell Honey she made Celebuphone. Good for her for keeping up with the highlights, what with the triplets and all.

"Sorry," Lola said to Doug, conspicuously setting her phone to vibrate.

"Are you ready to admit that you can't live without that thing?" Doug asked.

"I can't live without *this* thing," Lola said, pointing at Doug. Okay, that was awkward. Was that smile of his a little forced?

"Hey, guys," said Annabel.

"Hey! That is awesome," said Lola, admiring Annabel's cowgirl-style fringed suede skirt. "Where's Leo?"

Annabel opened her mouth, closed it, then opened it again.

"He doesn't go *everywhere* I go," said Annabel. "On dates, for example, not so much."

"We're not a date," said Lola.

"Yeah, but Ari is," said Annabel. "At ten."

"Oh, great!" Lola said.

Evidently, she wasn't too convincing.

"Lola, you can say it," Annabel said. "You're amused by my single antics, but you really want me to go out with Leo."

Whoa. Where did *that* come from?

"Well, the incident with Glassblower Guy *was* hilarious," said Lola.

Annabel didn't laugh.

"I—Bella, I want you to do whatever you want," said Lola.

Except publish a book based on your blog.

"Okay, but you think I *should* go out with Leo."

Yow. Clearly this has been brewing. Clearly I have been distracted.

"I don't know about *should*, I just think he's—"

"Sturdy? Dependable? Normal?" asked Annabel. "Lola, this isn't a book. Just because he's the 'great guy' who's 'right under my nose' doesn't mean I'm 'supposed' to be with him. Did it occur to you that I might just like him, but not *like* like him? Hmm, which advice columnist—former advice columnist—used to write about that stuff, telling people to not feel like they're being too 'picky' if they just don't feel it for someone 'terrific'? Oh wait. That was you."

Lola wanted to crawl into a bottle of grappa. Always the please-everyone only child, she hated getting in trouble—and above all, she hated fighting with her friends. In fact, she avoided it to the point that this was the first time she really remembered doing it. Even though Annabel was naturally more ornery than she was, she had the sense that this was big, big and awful, not like two kids on the playground who scream bloody murder at each other one second and play nice, all forgotten, the next. Lola didn't know how to do that. Or how to tell herself, "All right, she's angry; what can I learn from this?" Or what to say.

So Lola sat, cowed and silent.

"Lo, I don't know. You've been helpful and supportive on the outside, but still. I get this other vibe in there, too. It's been feeling like you're waiting for me to grow up and settle down, like you," said Annabel. "I know you guys don't have a den or anything, but still. I never thought it would happen," she said, shaking her head and taking a breath, "but I believe you've become a Smug Married."

That hit Lola where it hurt. Smack in the middle of her noblest intentions.

"But Annabel, I don't get it. It's not like I vanished, like, you know, everyone else, and got all uncool and 'we just don't have the energy for fun anymore.' I don't wax rhapsodic about how 'someday you'll understand.' Didn't we just have that talk about how everyone *else* is old? I still come out to parties and hang out with friends and—"

"Lo, it's not how you talk about you, it's how you talk about me," said Annabel. "To me. Besides, how well do I know you, Lola?"

Better than I want you to?

"It's not something specific that you did or said," Annabel went on. "It's something I can feel."

Then it hit Lola, sickening and sudden, like a wet, moldy gym towel someone snapped in her face. Annabel was right, but only half.

I *don't* want Annabel to "settle down"! I want to *want* her to. I want her right where she is, single and nutty, so I can be the sturdy one. I want her right where she is, so I can sit in judgment.

"Annabel, I—"

"I don't want to be mad at you, Lo. But I'm going to go be early for my date now, how crazy is that?" She drained her drink and left a ten on the bar. "I'll talk to you."

She kissed Lola on the cheek, said "Bye, Doug," and left.

Lola turned to Doug, helpless. He looked into his drink, then at his wife.

"Smug, I don't know," he said. "It's the married part that's bugging me."

Thirty-one

Lola stared.

Is he breaking up with me?

She knew she wasn't single anymore, but somehow, the same neurons were screaming "Mayday!" In any case, she was clearly in trouble.

With the two people I love most, is all.

"Doug? What do you mean?"

"I just—God, I hate to bombard you after all that . . ."

"No, no, go ahead," said Lola, signaling the bartender. "What, you should wait till I'm happy?"

"Well, I mean—and maybe in a weird way this is also related to what Annabel's feeling, so it seems maybe relevant . . . I just, it's like—uch, okay, I can't pretend this isn't bugging me anymore. It's that—especially since the murders, which I know has only been like a week—I never see you. Or like, even when I see you, I don't, really. Like at Coney. I feel like something should have shifted since then, but it hasn't," Doug said. He picked up his drink and absently wiped away the damp circle underneath. " 'Cause I know,

Lo, that you're doing anything you can to not talk about what I brought up the other day."

"The season finale of *24*?"

Doug didn't laugh.

Gah. For once, Lola, could you deactivate your Humor Defense Shields?

"Doug, I—"

"I know you love me, Lola. And I know being the easygoing good sport is, like, my thing. But I feel a bit . . . taken for granted. I know you're trying hard not to be swallowed into wifedom, making sure to see your friends and everything, but what advice columnist—"

"Former."

"Whatever. What advice columnist was always reminding readers that marriage isn't the holy grail; it's when the work *starts*?"

Lola, chastened, raised her hand. "Me?"

"Not like I think there's anything to *work* on, like anything's *wrong*. But, you know, plants need water."

"I know," said Lola. About that grappa bottle, she did feel just about small enough to crawl in. "I'm—"

"And it's not just the friends; it's work. Your work. I'm glad you have lots; that's great. It's not just the time you spend, though. It's this all-about-you persecution-complex ambition thing you have going on—it's, like, running you. I just feel it, like Annabel. Even more so—way more so—since the murders. It's like, your jaw is set so hard."

"Sweetie, I—"

"And while we're on the subject, why on earth was schlepping to the West Side Highway for a Tanqueray and tonic more important than date night at home?"

"I—" Lola began. Doug didn't interrupt her this time. "Well," Lola tried again, drawing a breath. "This may not be the most festive time to tell you that I made number three on the *New York Day* Chick Lit Bestseller list."

Or that the late Mimi McKee and Daphne Duplex were still holding steady in, respectively, places five and four. Right where they'd been the last time Lola checked, right after she'd met Destiny.

Thirty-two

"Whoa," said Doug. "I guess people do read those reviews! That's great, sweetie."

Lola was right, of course. It wasn't the best time. His tone was sweet, yet hollow, like those hard candies that melt into sharp edges that cut your tongue.

"Thanks," said Lola. She sighed. "And see, well, ugh, it feels so lame now, but I was so happy I wanted to come here because they serve free drinks to any writer on any bestseller list the day it comes out—and I'd just never had the chance—"

"Ah," said Doug.

"I just thought the scene might be a little more festive," said Lola. She looked around. Most of the scruffy characters lined up at the bar, hunched over amber-filled glasses, did look like writers. Specifically, writers in a Graham Greene screenplay about writers down on their luck.

Now I'm in a fix, she thought. I finally hatched a plot, and it's actually falling into place. I *really* need to try to do what I came here to do. *And* I could really use Doug as backup, but God, I so can't ask him now.

Or Annabel, of course.

Wow, am I alone right now.

"Sweetie, let me just go to the bathroom," Lola said. Compartmentalize, Somerville. Deal with horrible guilt and lameness later.

Her only ally at this point was, of all people, Wally Seaport. He—not even her mother!—was the first person she'd called after seeing the bestseller list.

"Thanks again for your help," Lola had said that morning, polishing off her second cup of coffee.

"Don't mention it," Wally replied.

"Actually, I was going to ask you to," she answered.

"Mention it?"

"Yes, please. On *Royalty*. Say I'll be at Earl's tonight. You know, the free drinks thingie," she said. "I know you don't owe me anything, but—oh, wait."

"Did you send me that cell phone?"

"I can neither confirm nor deny," Lola said flatly. She was enjoying this.

"Well, I was just about to follow up with this Destiny place about the murders, so thanks."

Lola smiled silently, spinning in her desk chair.

"Okay," Wally went on. "Are you sure you want me to post about you and Earl's? Have you ever—oh, I guess not. 'Cause really, it's—"

Lola interrupted. "I'm sure."

Bald-Faced Names
Posted by Page Proof

Jonesing for creamed spinach? Dreaming of meeting *Pink Slip* author/corpse magnet **Lola Somerville**, whose novel finally made an appearance on the *Day*'s Chick Lit list? Tonight you can satisfy both urges at Earl's, where *Royalty* hears that

Somerville, perhaps unaware that most writers play it cool and wait to hit the *Times* before collecting, will pop in for the free drinks she has technically now earned. For this drop-everything news, we thank our tipster ~~Lola Somerville~~ Hey, c'mon! *Royalty* never reveals its sources.

Ouch.
Figures.
Well.
Whatever it takes.

Lola did have to pat herself on the back when she got down to Earl's basement. Just as she'd remembered, it was dark, deserted, full of weird storerooms. There was certainly no one hanging out near the ladies' room—not so many ladies came here, after all. Good going, Somerville. You've laid the virtual bread crumbs; any chick lit killer in the know would follow the trail right here. This is indeed a good place for a murder.

Attempted murder.

Lola used the bathroom, dawdled at the scratched beveled mirror, listening for sounds. Nothing.

Back out into the hall. Nothing. No one.

What was that? She whirled around, catching her breath.

Still nothing.

Lola followed the hall to the end. EMERGENCY EXIT: ALARM WILL SOUND. Hmm. No way out but back up. Not the best getaway route. Maybe this is a bad place for a murder after all.

Or maybe this plan is utterly insane and will never work in a million years.

But while I'm here, let me take one more opportunity to make myself vulnerable. To the killer, not to my husband.

"Doug, this has all been a bit heady," Lola said, back at the bar.

"I'm just going to walk around the block for a minute—you know, clear my head, gather my thoughts. I know most women do this in the ladies' room, but that didn't quite do it. I'll come right back."

He hesitated for a moment. "Okay. But be careful. And then let's go home?"

"Sure," said Lola. "Yes, definitely." She kissed him on the cheek and squeezed his arm awkwardly. She was well aware that she—as before, and even now—had listened to and heard what Doug had to say, but they still hadn't had an actual *conversation* about it.

Okay. First this. Then that.

It will surely be that simple, as my plan is, once again, *insane*, and nothing will happen on this redonkulous killer-luring venture into the dark creepy streets of the west end of the meatpacking district.

Lola decided she'd give herself one trip around the block on which Earl's sat. She walked first toward the West Side Highway, past the one remaining pre-pashmina hourly rate hotel. Nothing. She rounded the corner and walked, illuminated only by headlights, along the highway, hulking aqueducts lining its far side along the Hudson. Farther ahead, on the next block, she could see some large fellows spilling out of The Choke, the only biker bar left in Manhattan that hadn't been made into a movie.

Okay, she thought as she turned right again, I covered the waterfront.

The block she was now on was deserted, smelling of salt, bike exhaust, and possibly pee.

Lola's phone beeped. She started.

I got a message? When did it even ring?

Lola dug the phone out of her bag.

Maybe it's Annabel.

Please let it be Annabel, but only if she's calling to take it all back.

Text message.

9:24 PM, uptowngal, Molly Ringwald at Mood Ring, rather
upset

Ooh! That's right around the corner. I'd love to see how her
hair is—

Someone stepped out from behind a Dumpster.

Suddenly, Lola was face-to-face with Reading Guy.

Locking his huge magnified bug eyes with hers, he finally
spoke.

"You're next," he said.

Thirty-three

This time, Lola did not contemplate the relative merits of backing away slowly. She turned on her heel and sprinted. Next time, she thought, remind me not to wear clogs to a getaway.

Fortunately, The Choke was close by. Lola knew she'd be safe once back on terra biker bar, considering that most of its customers also worked as bouncers. And indeed, she reached the gleaming rows of motorcycles before she'd even had a chance to look back.

Now, though, she did.

And Reading Guy was gone.

"You all right?"

Lola whirled back around. An extremely tan woman in a jean jacket and leather pants was leaning on a motorcycle, cigarette in one hand, pen in the other. The wisp of curling smoke wove past her long feather earrings and into her wavy brown hair.

"Oh, me? Oh, yeah, I'm fine, thanks," said Lola, waving a hand dismissively. Yeah. Now ask me about my marriage. And my best friendship.

She stood there another moment to catch her breath. The

woman nodded and wrote something down. Lola glanced at the notebook balanced on the motorcycle seat.

"Are—are you a reporter?" she asked.

"Oh, no." The woman smiled. "I mean, not really. A writer. I'm writing a book about being a female biker. You know, a memoir."

Of course you are.

"And my editor—"

Editor? This isn't just in the idea phase? The permanent idea phase?

"—wanted even more, what'd she call it, 'real immediacy' in the bar scenes, so. Just stepped out here to take some notes."

"I'll watch for it," smiled Lola. "What's it called?"

The woman grinned, showing straight but browned teeth, and pointed down to a sticker on her bike. Which read, If You Can Read This, the Bitch Just Passed You.

Lola had to laugh. "Well, good luck, um—"

"Delilah."

"Delilah. I'm Lola. Good luck."

"You, too, Lola. You have a good one," said Delilah. She looked down. "And next time, be careful running in those."

Lola waved as she hurried toward Earl's. The encounter with Delilah—and, actually, with Reading Guy—had buoyed Lola, if slightly. One, it appeared that her plan had worked: she had not only smoked out the killer but also (bonus!) had boosted book sales in the process, and two, this she had confirmed: you gotta get a gimmick. Biking worked for Delilah, Lola thought; maybe sleuthing really was going to work for me.

Now to face my husband.

And then, my best friend.

Taking a breath, Lola walked back into Earl's.

She found Doug chatting with the bartender.

"No, actually, the other way around: it's the *even* Star Trek films that are good, and the *odd* Nightmare on Elm Streets," Doug was saying, a bit wearily.

Lola mustered a smile. "You ready?"

"Yep," he said, fishing a ten out of his wallet. Nice tip. Nice Doug. "Thanks, man."

He turned to Lola, nodding back at the bartender. "We bonded."

She linked her arm in his as they left. She knew he liked that.

For the first five minutes of the cab ride, they sat in silence. As far as Lola could remember, it was also the first five minutes of silence of their relationship.

In her heart of hearts, she actually felt that Doug was being a tad petulant. This trait of his surfaced now and then, and Lola believed it had to do with the fact that he had three siblings. That old chestnut about only children needing constant attention, even into adulthood? Backwards. We *had* constant attention, she thought. It's the people with siblings who had to fight for it—and sometimes still feel like they do.

At the same time, she was mortified. Right or wrong, Doug was upset with her—he felt she had let him down—and this she could hardly bear. And given that the plot she was involved in was only thickening, she wasn't about to do anything except beg forgiveness for what she had wrought so far. As soon as she could think of what to say. And as soon as she could get what had happened with Reading Guy out of her head.

The cabbie broke the silence. Lola hadn't even noticed that the driver was a woman. This was not common.

"So, you guys writers?" she asked. "I just figured, what with Earl's, Brooklyn . . ."

Not now, lady cabdriver, Lola thought.

"No no," Doug said, coming to the rescue. "Computer stuff."

"Oh, even better," said the driver. "Maybe you can tell me how to start a blog. You know, about being a lady cabdriver. My agent—"

Lola pretended she hadn't heard. "Listen, Doug."

I've successfully lured the killer with myself as bait, which was both inspired and idiotic. Which is what I really want to tell you, but I can't because of the "idiotic" part.

"Listen, I—I think what's really bothering me, beneath everything, and part of why I'm acting so weird, other than the fact that I've discovered two bodies in two days and"—lie—"haven't gotten all that far with helping my friend find the killer, is . . . I just don't think I'm ready yet to have a baby."

"Oh," said Doug.

The cabdriver didn't press the blog issue.

"I've been dodging it because I so hate to disappoint you. Disappointing you is, like, physically painful." Now she was telling the truth. "I just don't feel secure enough yet. I mean, not with you. I mean, stable. In my own life. But I do want kids, and I do want kids with you. That's not a question. And I promise I'm not waiting for some magical day to come that never will. Soon," said Lola. "I will be ready soon." Soon as the rest of my life falls into place. Or just one little next big thing. She took his hand.

The cabdriver turned up the smooth jazz.

Doug nodded. "That's okay, monkey. I mean, I can't force you—"

"Other than by secretly replacing my birth control pills with Tic Tacs," said Lola.

"Hmm!" said Doug, arching his eyebrows and tapping together his fingertips, evil genius style. "No, seriously, Lo, it just feels better to have cleared the air. Thanks for saying something."

They made out the rest of the way home. But Lola knew they were both distracted, and not just because Doug kept having to surface to give directions. Or because Lola kept interrupting their lip-lock to fill Doug in on stuff he'd missed.

"Oh, Annabel sold a book based on her blog. That's what I was helping her with the other day."

"Mmm," said Doug, corralling her mouth with his. "Great. I mean, shit."

"Mmmmsokay." It felt good to kiss Doug. It always felt good to kiss Doug. But the many parts of her brain that weren't saying "kissing . . . Doug . . . nice" were still racing.

I must now put all of my energy into plotting my next move—proving Reading Guy's guilt—not getting killed, and making it look like none of this is more important than my marriage, or my best friendship, Lola thought. Which, at the end of the day, it isn't. It's just more . . . urgent.

"Right up here, just ahead of that hydrant," Doug said. He glanced at the meter while it clicked and buzzed. As he got out his wallet, the DJ came on the radio.

"Overnight and tomorrow, continued mild, with air quality better than L.A., but not as good as Taos."

"Just go to the website Blogger.com," Doug told the driver, handing over some bills. "You can use one of their free templates."

"Hey, thanks!" she replied. Lola was halfway out the door.

"And now, some breaking news," said the radio. "Writer Honey Porter, whose book is due out next week, collapsed inside Bergdorf's this evening after having her trademark blond hair touched up during the new extended hours at the store's world-famous, and recently renovated, spa and salon. EMTs arriving quickly on the scene, fresh from treating victims of the stampede across the street at FAO Schwartz for the pregnant Jennifer Aniston action figure, were unable to revive her."

Thirty-four

Lola collapsed onto the bed.

Honey's dead.

Is it my fault?

Did Reading Guy go off and kill Honey somehow after—that is, *because* I—embarrassingly easily, foiled his attempt to kill me? How could he have known where she was? He's the kind of guy who would carry a transistor radio in his bike basket—could he actually have Celebuphone? And even if he did, how'd he get to midtown so fast?

At the very least, Lola thought, so much for my genius theory about the murders following the order of the bestseller list. Or having anything to do with me.

And so much for Annabel's respect. Not to mention my vow of complete honesty with my husband.

What have I done?

Lola squeezed her eyes shut and rubbed her temples.

"Monkey, let me get you something," said Doug. "Egg noodles? Sleepytime? Cuervo Gold?"

"Honey," Lola murmured.

"Yeah?" Doug said. "Oh, duh. Sorry. Honey as in Porter." He sighed and climbed into bed next to Lola and lay down, knees up. They both faced the ceiling. "Just let me know if you decide you want something."

"Thanks," Lola said. "Those triplets . . ."

"You want to adopt Honey's triplets?"

"No. God, sorry. I'm too spent for segues. I just meant, those poor triplets."

"I know," sighed Doug. "It's even worse than Daphne's dogs. Say, Lola?"

She turned her head on the pillow.

"Don't you think it's about time?" he asked.

"To have babies?" Lola asked, her eyes wide. That was fast.

"No, shit, sorry. Wow, our usual communication skills are just not up to par right now, are they?"

Lola felt a dull thud between her ribs. She said nothing.

"I mean, time for you to drop the case? I was into it when you said it was pretty much a desk job, but now I'm not so sure. That I'm into it, or that it's really a desk job. Unless you have a new desk on the corner outside Earl's," he said. "Once I thought about it, it was pretty clear what you were up to. Though, thankfully—not that it wasn't clever!—the killer seemed to have been busy in midtown."

Even as she winced, Lola felt a glimmer of admiration. Her husband was so damn smart.

"I just—not like it was fun when it was only Mimi, but Lo, three people are dead, and the killer, if it is just one killer, is on the loose," Doug went on. "You're very capable, and you're pretty obsessive, and compulsive, but you're not Monk. You're not a detective. You're a writer. And I'm your husband. And I worry. And, as you know, I miss you. I know I can't tell you what to do, and I've read enough of your articles about relationships to know that I should use 'I statements,' so here goes: *I* am worried about you getting in too deep with this thing, and *I* would like things to go back to the way they were between us, with nothing hidden and nothing weird, so *I* would be very happy if you would wait until it's over and *then* write about it, like Sebastian Junger."

"Actually, he's totally covered, like, the war in Bosnia and big wildfires, plus once when he was working as a tree trimmer he almost cut off his leg with a chain saw," said Lola. She paused. "Okay, I will."

What am I saying?

"Wait. 'Okay?'" said Doug. "You'll quit?"

"Yes." *What I am saying is that I'll say anything to avoid conflict.*

"*Quit* quit?"

"I'll . . . keep tabs. You know, read Gawker, text Quentin if I see anything interesting."

"You'll text?" Doug was delighted. "Like, send a text message, not just receive, from your fancy phone that you hate and have heretofore refused to text-message from, even though it's equipped with the super-easy QWERTY keyboard?"

Lola nodded and smiled. *She knew that would work.*

And that she, quite possibly, had never sunk lower.

The phone rang. *Please let it be Annabel. Please let her announce that she'd freed herself from the sci-fi mind control exercised by that playboy neurologist with the offshore medical degree that she'd dated once or twice, and that she took back everything she'd said at Earl's.*

Or at least let it be Bobbsey, phoning to say he'd missed her at the murder scene. And that he'd caught the killer, so that things could go back to nice, albeit book-deal-free, and normal.

"No, you're right, she's not pregnant," Lola heard Doug say out in the hall.

Huh?

"That's why her people recalled the pregnant doll, which is why it immediately became so valuable."

Oh.

Doug came into the room with the phone and his laptop. "Lo, it's your mom." He climbed into bed with Lola and passed her the phone.

"Oh good, you're home," said Mrs. Somerville. "I heard. I'm so sorry, Lulu. Wasn't she a friend of yours?"

"Yes, Mommy," Lola whimpered.

And some friend I am. Was.

"Oh, sweetie. I'm so sorry. Do you want me to get on the shuttle?"

"No, thanks, Mom. I've got Doug," Lola said. He smiled. Shit.

"Of course you do," said her mom. "And you don't dye your hair anymore, do you?"

"No, Mom." Only with some sort of organic vegetable stuff, if you must know.

"Good. You know. Phthalates."

"I know."

"And antiperspirant's no good, either."

"I know, Mom. Listen, thanks for calling. I think I'm gonna try to get some sleep for once," said Lola.

"Not before you read this," said Doug, passing Lola his laptop.

Thirty-five

Femi-Nabbed!

Posted by Page Proof

A notorious overall-clad feminist activist is being questioned aggressively in conjunction with the apparent murder of writer Honey Porter, 36, a curvy single mother of young triplets. Wilma Vouch, founder and leader of the Jane Austen Liberation Front, whose members are a common—and angry—presence outside readings and parties for books of the popular chick lit genre, had, curiously, no comment as she was led into a midtown precinct station house. Ms. Vouch had reportedly been spotted in Bergdorf's—the site of Ms. Porter's demise—which, as bystanders who tipped off the police averred, could itself be considered suspicious for a woman of her grooming.

Ms. Porter's death has not officially been ruled a homicide. NYPD detective Bradley Bobbsey did confirm, however, that the police are working under the assumption that the writer's untimely demise is linked to the recent murders of fellow chick lit authors Mimi McKee and Daphne Duplex. Though Ms. Duplex's killing took place in Brooklyn, the authorities are currently assuming that it still counts.

Ms. Porter was found unconscious earlier this evening inside Bergdorf's, where, amid the stares of tourists who were heard to murmur excitedly, "They must be filming *Law and Order!*" she soon died. She had apparently just come from her regular appointment with famed androgynous colorist Luna, who sobbed over her body as it was taken away. "What a waste!" Luna wailed at the scene. "Delicate ribbons of flax had been intertwined with streaks of vanilla and threads of gold strategically placed over a honey-toned base!"

Luna has been questioned by the police but is apparently not considered a suspect.

Ms. Porter was not known to have any health problems that might predispose her to sudden collapse or death, said a family spokesperson who declined to be identified. While there were no visible signs of foul play, investigators quickly confirmed that no other customer at Bergdorf's salon that evening had been similarly overcome. A full report on the cause of death could take up to a week, they added.

The police have not confirmed why Ms. Vouch appears to have been singled out as the prime—indeed, the only—suspect in this murder, and perhaps by extension, the others. Some of her detractors were, however, willing to hazard a tentative guess. "Who the hell else would have done it?" wondered firebrand commentatress Alexandria Coltish, author of the best-selling books *Shut Up, Liberals: For Chrissake, Shut Up*, and *La La La Not Listening.* "See what happens when women get angry?"

Lola looked up at the ceiling. She just couldn't stomach the rest.

On the upside, if Wilma is the killer, I may not be responsible for Honey's death, much as I may have secretly, fleetingly pretend-wished for it at Oona's shower.

However, the downsides are not excellent either. One, if it is Wilma, which I swear to God I thought of before Bobbsey did, I have wasted my time with Reading Guy and will get no credit whatsoever. Two, it turns out that someone whose book hasn't been out long enough for major sales figures to register is seen as a worthier target than me. Three, a feminist perp is pretty much the worst PR possible for the women's movement. In which case, on top of everything, I must remember to increase my financial contributions to NOW.

Four, Annabel is mad at me. I know this is unrelated, but I can't get it out of my head.

"Well, there you go," said Doug, finishing the article.

"Yep," said Lola. "*If* she did it."

"God, my iBook looks hot on your lap," Doug said drowsily.

Lola reached for his hand, then remembered. "Shoot, my mom asked me to call her right back." She reached instead for the phone.

"Well, now that you're up to speed, there's another reason I'm upset," said Mrs. Somerville.

Oh God. What did I do? What does she know? The kid-in-trouble neurons, despite their thirty-two years, were—like those breakup neurons—still always *thisclose* to firing.

"What, Mom?"

"It's about Wilma," said Mrs. Somerville. "I know she didn't do it."

Thirty-six

"Wilma and I go way back, back to the days of protesting *Deep Throat*," Mrs. Somerville explained. "Of course I was three at the time."

"Wait, what?"

"Lulu, I'm kidding."

"Sorry, Mom. I'm just trying to keep my head from exploding." Lola passed the laptop back to Doug. "Why hadn't you ever told me?"

"Well, she's actually still a client," said Mrs. Somerville. "I'm supposed to keep those things on the low-down, or the down-low, or whatever you call it."

"You're kidding."

"This time, no," said Lola's mom. "And I know she's not guilty of murder."

"Just not capable of it, huh?" asked Lola.

"Oh no, Wilma'd rip your throat out in a heartbeat," said her mother. "I just know she didn't do *this*."

"How?"

"I . . . just do."

"Well, can you do something? Say something?"

"I'd rather wait and see her released for lack of evidence than do anything that would threaten our confidentiality agreement." Mrs. Somerville sighed. "Even so, this could be a major setback for her. She was doing so well at journaling through her rage."

"Wow, Mom," said Lola.

"Guess all we can do in the meantime is double our contributions to NOW."

"Yeah, I thought of that," said Lola.

"Lulu, you'll keep this under your hat, won't you?"

"Of course, Mom."

"You do wear a hat, don't you?"

"Of course, Mommy."

Lola got ready for bed feeling vaguely better. Quentin had e-mailed to say he'd been glad to hear the news about Wilma—at least she wouldn't feel such acute pressure to come through for him right now. Doug, poor thing, had drifted off with his glasses on and his hands on his iBook, itself asleep. Lola gently removed both and tucked him in.

I know things will be okay, she thought. I just have to be careful. I trust my mom's professional instincts a hundred percent, less so the cops' interest in speedily clearing Wilma's name. This could buy me a bit more time, Lola thought, to track down the real killer. Then mom's happy, Wilma's happy, Quentin's happy, I'm happy: everybody wins. Except Detective Bobbsey.

Well, that was easy, Lola thought, adjusting the covers. Now, what about Annabel?

Okay, I can think about her for five minutes, and then, when I roll over to my other side, I have to stop.

Lola thought about Annabel.

She rolled over.

Lola kept thinking about Annabel.

With a mystery, I can more or less make my own way. And I'm fine with friendships as long as they're . . . fine. But this one, right now, I just don't know how to fix.

Finally drifting off, Doug snoring softly next to her, Lola slipped into an unpleasant dream. She was trapped, squinting and blinking, in some too-bright place, some place with an acrid, almost burnt-coffee smell, some place where she felt she didn't belong but yet, for some reason, had to be. She walked down carpeted aisles with no end, picking up speed as her discomfort increased, then recoiling as her toe touched one body sprawled on the floor, then another. Her heart raced. A rumbling behind her made her turn her head. Rolling down the aisle toward her, like the boulder in *Indiana Jones*, was a giant blueberry scone. Lola ran. She opened her mouth to scream. Nothing came out.

Lola woke up in a damp sweat. She touched Doug's arm gently, then drew back. When morning came, she now knew, her quest would have to take her to its scariest place yet.

Thirty-seven

There were few places that frightened Lola more than the bookstore.

Well, not just any bookstore. Primarily the megastore Starbooks, which had in fact gulped most other bookstores, and even a couple of libraries, into its heaving maw. (Ironically, though, Starbooks had served as a great boon to gay bookstores ever since the uproar over the chain's refusal to stock the book *Daddy's Roommate*.)

Despite neighborhood protest, a new Starbooks had just opened in downtown Brooklyn amid the Foot Lockers and fried chicken joints. Like the others in the chain, it also sold CDs, DVDs, reading-related accessories—bookmarks, lamps, chairs—and, at the café, baked goods marked with their respective trans-fat content and "Staruccinos" in suspicious flavors such as tiramisu and country peach. The Brooklyn store's claim to fame was that two employees had recently gotten married in its central aisle, which may have had something to do with the fact that the store's construction had required mowing down a church.

So Lola feared Starbooks' global domination plan, not to mention its bagels, and also the unbecoming feelings that any bookstore provoked in her. Normally, when she'd venture in on perverse impulse, she'd find her books on the shelf, which was great, except they'd be the same three books she'd seen on the shelf the last time she'd checked. (She'd leave a small crease on a back page as evidence for her return trip.) And then, of course, she'd see everyone else's books enjoying pride of place on an end-of-aisle rack or some sort of exciting "customer favorites" display.

Maybe today, with her moment on the *Day*'s bestseller list, would be better.

Of course, today hadn't started off so great in other ways, Lola thought as she walked past the cement-and-wire juvie prison whose lower floors were currently being transformed into retail shops. Doug had gone off to Tekserve, leaving the other half of his banana sliced in a cereal bowl for Lola. ("I wasn't sure when you'd be up!" he'd said, pecking her on the cheek. "And . . . not sure when I'll be home. I think I'm gonna meet Chris and Colin—the Old Bathhouse is showing *Shaolin Soccer* in 3-D. Stay out of trouble, 'kay?") Boy, did he look cute when he wore a button-down that wasn't a bowling shirt. Or did I notice his shirt 'cause I can't hold his gaze?

Lola watered her plants, then set off for the long, hopefully head-clearing walk to downtown. Even Reading Guy, it seemed, had joined Annabel in the Avoiding Lola Club. While she felt fairly confident that Reading Guy wouldn't attempt to stalk her in broad daylight, she also felt, when she looked back and saw no one behind her, more alone than ever.

She passed Four Franks, the famous storefront restaurant known for its mob connections and lack of printed menu. What they had that night, you ate. The dinner she had had there with Annabel, not too long ago, was the only time Lola had ever eaten veal, because she'd been afraid to say no to the waiter.

Annabel. On impulse, Lola dialed from her cell, mostly hoping her friend wouldn't pick up, unless of course she were to pick up and say, "Lo, I take it all back. I know now that I was a victim of absinthe."

Voice mail.

"Bella, it's me. I'm just—I suck. Call me back. I mean, if you want." Lola paused, then hung up.

Bravissima! That was pathetic.

Lola put her phone away, making sure the ringer was set to Loud.

As she pushed open the door of Starbooks, Lola noticed right away that she was among a minority of people entering the store on foot. Strollers everywhere, all going the same way like some sort of Bugaboo wagon train. Lola craned her neck. Over in the kids' section, she could make out the tips of some white rabbit ears on a furrily costumed grown-up, likely a graduate of Juilliard's drama program trying to make a living, and likely there for an event promoting the upcoming release of *Pat the Bunny: The Movie.*

Can I really bring a child into this world?

Lola took a step toward the chick lit section, then stopped.

Well, that's handy.

The books I'm looking for should all be right here on this new display.

Lola approached the table near the front whose sign usually read something like Hot Beach Reads! or Everything Da Vinci! Today, it read Murdered Authors.

Lola quickly found Mimi's, Daphne's, and Honey's books among a few apparent murdered-author afterthoughts: Marlowe's *Doctor Faustus* and a couple of works by dissident intellectuals.

Let's think. Who stands to profit from these deaths? Starbooks, sure, but nefarious as they are, its hard to believe they'd hire assassins. The authors' agents? Lola knew the three women did not share an agent or a publisher. What else could they have in common?

Grabbing copies of her friends' books, she went looking for a chair. The bookstore's Biography and Emeril Lagasse sections were too crowded, but Lola found an empty seat in Current Events. As she settled into the crumb-flecked chair, someone caught her eye.

It was Blanca Palette, with some really lovely new auburn

highlights. But she didn't look as good as her hair. Sniffling slightly, she was pulling her books out of the chick lit section and placing them in the crook of her arm.

Oh no, Lola thought. Has she resorted to buying them all herself to boost sales?

More likely, of course, is that she's bringing them up to the front desk so she can sign them and get them affixed with Signed By Author stickers, which could help a bit with sales. It always struck Lola as funny that when she went in to ask to sign her books, no one ever seemed to double-check her face against her author photo. She'd always wondered what would happen if she came in and asked to sign Alexander Haig's autobiography, say.

Watching Blanca turn away, Lola was struck by a hunch. She set her reading project down on her seat and tiptoed after Blanca, her steps muffled by the store's ambient music, which appeared to be Andrea Bocelli's earsplitting duet with Elmo. Sure enough, Blanca took a left into the literary fiction section and seemed to go straight to a familiar spot. Calmly, like a practiced criminal, she set her books on the shelf, facing out, and walked briskly off. Lola waited a beat, then took a look. Sure enough, there they sat, under P, between Paletta and Palevsky, in their rightful literary place.

Poor Blanca.

Lola found her chair still empty and picked up her books again. She wasn't sure what she was looking for. She just knew that police-work-wise, she was at a loss: utterly confused by recent events with Reading Guy, unsure of how to proceed with the Wilma defense. That's why she had a strong urge to turn, for her next step, to what she did know: books. Could these three departed authors have more in common than a literary genre? Lola wondered. And, simply by doing a close reading, could I be the one to uncover it?

Let's see. Should I start in murder order or alpha by first name? Lola selected the less creepy option and opened Daphne's book.

Half an hour later, she was still engrossed—and more than halfway done.

This is actually pretty good, Lola thought, stopping for a moment to stretch. Poor Daphne.

She turned a page. Then another. And then, frowning, she read that same page again.

No way.

She read the section one more time to be sure.

Yep, it's there.

Can this possibly be a coincidence?

Thirty-eight

I was in his remarkably clean bathroom, putting in my contacts, thanking God that I'd finally gotten mature enough to realize that traveling with saline solution was not so much slutty as practical, when I heard a sudden and rather dramatic yelp from the kitchen.

What could be the matter? Had Max just realized he'd made decaf instead of regular? Had he been bested by Lianne Hansen on the Morning Edition word puzzle? Had he realized he wished that last night, though not much had happened, had never happened?

I was curious to know what was wrong, of course, but I also really wanted to be out of there already. Just because I'd stayed over at his apartment didn't mean I knew how I felt about him; it simply meant that I lived in Brooklyn.

So into the kitchen I went, still blind in one contactless eye, to see what had happened.

"Hey, you okay?" I asked.

Far as I could make out, Max was sitting on a kitchen stool, gripping its sides, staring at the open door under his sink.

"Can you do me a favor?" he asked. He sounded terribly rattled.

"Does it require binocular vision?" I asked.

"Can you get rid of the mouse under the sink?"

It all sounded crazily, impossibly familiar. There was just one salient difference.

With my useless eye closed, I took a piece of paper towel, used it to remove the poor dead mouse from the "humane" trap, dropped it into a blue *New York Times* bag, walked it all the way down to the trash can on the street, washed my hands, and put in my other contact, thinking all the while, "Now, *this* is a man who's not afraid to show that he's vulnerable."

I walked back into the kitchen, smiling, and took Max's hand.

"Brooklyn can wait," I purred. "Let's go back to bed."

Lola shut the book, her head spinning. How could Daphne have come up with that? Aside from the, uh, happier ending, the rest of the scene was, play by play, practically line by line, exactly what had happened between Lola and Quentin that infamous mousy morning.

Had Quentin told Daphne? He must have, except for the part where Lola was fairly sure the two of them had never met. Even at Mimi's side, he wasn't quite far enough up the fabulous food chain. I mean sure, maybe they met at a party, maybe it just came up, maybe the story—in uncanny detail?—just made its way into Daphne's book.

Or could Quentin have told Mimi, and Mimi told Daphne? Either could be true, but why? Lola couldn't imagine Quentin boasting about the real story or lying about the fake one. It wasn't Quentin's style, and at the end of the day, with either ending, it just wasn't *that* good a story.

No, the Quentin/mouse story was hardly the stuff of urban legend, and even if it were, it would never have been passed along in such accurate detail. And Lola's spider sense told her that its strange and ninety-nine percent accurate appearance in the book was more than an idle coincidence.

Really, Lola thought, this comes back down to Daphne, who is dead. And Quentin, who is not.

And whose entire hard drive is in my house.

Thirty-nine

This time, Lola decided, I'll take the damn bus.

She waited on the corner of Atlantic and Ledger, hands shoved in her jean-skirt pockets, tapping her clog.

C'mon, bus.

Lola stared at the ad on the side of the small Plexiglas shelter.

Sweet Nothings, it read. Two Sisters. One Calorie. No Shame.

Swell, Lola thought. The ridiculous Crystal girls get their own reality show, I get to wait for the bus.

She stepped out of the shelter and looked down the street.

C'mon, bus. Detective Somerville's got a lead to follow.

She leafed through the rest of Daphne's book, which she'd forced herself to buy, but found no other mysterious passages at first glance. She tried to scan the others but just couldn't get herself to concentrate.

C'mon, bus.

Of course, if I were Doug, I'd do *something* useful while I'm standing here, like use my fancy phone to check e-mail or surf the Web.

Also, if I were Doug, I'd hate me.

C'mon, bus.

Laughter erupted behind her. Turning, Lola saw a pack of stroller-pushing moms in vintage granny-style glasses and T-shirts with cracked iron-ons that said things like Free Winona and Quispy, Quunchy, Quazy Energy Cereal, their children shaded from the fierce sun with mini–trucker caps. They were heading for a newish-looking bar called Grup, sandwiched between a knitting store and a bail bonds joint. Lola, puzzled, glanced at the blackboard easel sitting on the sidewalk outside the bar: Liquid Play Date, it read. 2 for 1 'til 2 PM.

C'mon, bus. C'mon, book deal. The sooner I get my life in order, the sooner *I* can enjoy a liquid play date.

Lola glanced down the avenue again, then the opposite direction. Are buses even, like, running? Is there a strike I don't know about?

Wait, was that—?

Lola squinted into the sun, dimly aware that with her level of myopia, which could lead to macular degeneration, she was supposed to wear sunglasses in all seasons and take a daily dose of lutein.

Yep. That was Leo's Escarole, coming down the far side of the street.

Boy, could I use a ride. Was that Leo driving?

Lola waved tentatively. As she strained to see, she thought she noticed the SUV slow down a bit as she entered its sights.

Oh, awesome.

But then, just as fast, it accelerated and sped away. Just as it passed, Lola saw Leo's face, staring straight ahead, behind the wheel. And someone else in the passenger seat.

Annabel.

Must have been.

Ouch.

Wounded, Lola blinked back tears.

C'mon, bus.

Lola moped for the whole ride from downtown to NoWay, her concentration on her hurt feelings broken only once, by a five-year-old girl in tiny Ugg boots howling for "another cappuccino."

"That's *enough!*" hissed her weary mother, flylike in her giant sunglasses. "Do you want to wind up in Metropolitan Diary?"

Once home, Lola made herself shake off the sulk and get to work. Back in her office, she poured herself some seltzer and attached Doug's minidrive, which held Quentin's hard drive—and, hopefully, *something* to go on—to her computer. The Mac clicked and whirred obediently.

Let's see.

Lola opened a folder marked Puzzles. Sure enough, puzzles. She clicked around a bit, but nothing leapt out.

Hmm. How about Misc.? Feh. Just some drafts of a speech Quentin had given at some sort of puzzle writers' convention.

Browser history. Lola clicked, deathly afraid she'd find links to naked photos of Alexandria Coltish.

Well. Quentin was apparently a fan of Annabel's blog. Harrumph. But other than that, she found mostly links to obscure reference sources on military history, rare fauna, and famous shipwrecks—work stuff, must be. Ah, and here was a directory of baby names—surely Zoe would be a handy Z word? Xander could also be of use.

Sucked in, Lola searched one particular baby name site for "Lola," though she knew the answer already. "Spanish: sorrowful." Just for once, couldn't one resource say "Welsh: wildly successful" or at least "Persian: forgivable"?

A name that meant *sorrowful* indeed seemed an odd choice for the generally cheerful Somerville family. In fact, Lola had been named for her father's older brother Laszlo, whom Lola remembered only dimly. An avid athlete and healthy eater who had smoked about twice, like, ever, Uncle Laszlo had succumbed far too young to lung cancer, which had *really* crossed Lola's mother's worry wires.

Suddenly sentimental, Lola found her eyes wandering to an ad in the website's margins that featured a photo of a supercute baby hatching from a giant egg.

Eggspirationdate.com? Lola clicked.

Oh, dear.

"YOUR TIME IS RUNNING OUT!"

The cute baby was gone. Instead, giant red letters flashed against a black screen.

"YOUR TIME IS RUNNING OUT!"

"YOUR TIME IS RUNNING OUT!"

Warily, Lola scrolled down.

"We know you're busy. Busy focusing on your career, your fun, your desire to live in the moment, your search for a great guy who's worthy of forever. But do you know what your eggs are doing while you're so busy? They're *spoiling*, if not running out entirely. And do you know where that's going to leave you when—if!—you finally get around to trying to get pregnant? Busy . . . being *barren*.

"Fortunately, we are here to help. Click on the links at right for testimonials by women who wised up just in time; information about invasive, expensive, last-ditch fertility treatments; and our Internet dating partner, Good-Enough.com."

Lola wiped her brow. Ye gods, was that a bead of sweat?

I am *not* going to hurry up and breed just out of fear, she resolved. That can't be good for the baby.

Though now I really am a little scared, she thought. Sorrowful, maybe even. Why? Because that damn site awakened my true—and bereft—maternal instincts? Or because I'm one of the lucky ones who found someone "worthy," but he and I are not in a very baby place right now? Even though my most recent actions might have led him to believe we're closer?

Lola squeezed her eyes shut and quit Quentin's browser altogether.

Focus, Somerville, focus.

Okay. Okay. Think.

What's left?

Quentin's e-mail archives.

Lola clicked.

Hell's bells.

I'm going to need his password.

Lola noodled around Quentin's internal settings, searching for any sort of clue or perhaps a handy document marked List of Quentin's Passwords.

Eureka!

I am a genius, thought Lola. She'd dug up the list of passwords stored by his Web browser.

Going back to his e-mail, she tried them one by one.

Not one of them worked.

Goddamn it.

Lola leaned back in her chair, letting out a long breath. There's only one thing I can do right now, she thought. And it's really, really bad.

Forty

"Dougie, I need your help." Lola had the phone propped between her ear and shoulder. "I know you're busy over there. I'm sorry."

"Of course, monkey, no problem. I actually have a couple minutes right now. Do you need Help as in 'I need your input on this life decision' help, or help as in—"

"Tech support," said Lola.

"Even better," said Doug.

"I'm—I'm trying to help Sylvie—you know Sylvie, the editor?—anyway, I'm trying to help her open something she sent to Web mail for safekeeping. Only now she's forgotten the password, and she needs it. Much as I have learned from you, this is beyond my hacking ability."

There. She'd done it. The biggest, most specific lie she'd ever told Doug. The second biggest, but more vague—and only other one—had been the night before.

Who *am* I? How did I let it come to this? Is my future, my career, my ego really so important? Why am I willing to betray Doug's trust? Why do I feel like I'm cheating on him?

I have crossed a line.

Lola felt a caving in her chest, like one of those sinkholes on Third Avenue that could swallow a bus. Only she also felt something else around the edges: a dim buzzing, a fuzzy rush.

Am I actually getting a *thrill* out of this?

See you in hell, serial killer.

"Stay and help you I will," said Doug.

Now or never, Somerville. Rather: now, or later, when he'll be much further past the point of understanding.

Lola took a breath. "Find your friend, hmmm?" she said, trying to match Doug's best Yoda.

"I love you. Love you I. Whatever," said Doug.

He talked Lola into the right screen and they hunkered down. "<input type=HIDDEN name='FORM_SUBMIT_EMAIL_submit' value=," he dictated. "Okay, then put in her e-mail address."

Her? Lola thought. Oh, right. I'm lying.

Lola typed, and clicked, and typed some more, giving herself a chance every moment to stop and admit her transgression. And, every moment, not taking it.

"Okay, now Return," said Doug.

Click.

She was in.

"Doug, you rule."

"Strong is Vader. Mind what you have learned."

Lola grinned. "You are the biggest geek in the world."

"No," said Doug. "There is another."

Lola howled with laughter. "I'll see you later."

Assuming I can look you in the eye.

Lola scrolled through Quentin's e-mail, noting, with some sadness, that of course it all dated back to when Mimi was alive. Lola found several exchanges with her, naturally, but she could tell by glancing at them that they were just banter, plan-making, silly forwards. A handful were work-related, crossword stuff. There was also a receipt from Eddie Bauer, a notice from eBay that Quentin had been outbid for a 1948 Joe DiMaggio card, #1, PSA 8 NM/MT, whatever that meant, for which the higher bid was $6,702.50. *Whoa.* Guess that's the kind of thing you save up for. Like Doug and his Buck Rogers disintegrator gun, with holster, or his Batman handcuffs that had become extremely expensive collectors' items when they were recalled after it turned out, hazardously enough, that they actually worked. Doug was so proud of his Batcuffs that he'd never opened them; "mint on card" condition, they called it.

Anyway.

Fuck.

Lola leaned her head back and ran her fingers through her hair, pulling just hard enough to make it start to hurt.

Whole lotta nothing.

I *lied* to Doug for a whole lotta nothing.

Lola swung her head forward and banged Command-Q. Quit.

Now what? Now what the hell do I do?

As Lola raised her head, something in Quentin's Documents folder caught her eye.

A subfolder marked Other. But I looked at that, right?

Lola scanned down. No. I looked at Misc.

Why would you have a Misc. *and* an Other? Lola wondered, annoyed by this apparent organizational excess. She clicked on Other for the hell of it, with half a mind to merge the two files, just for her own compulsive benefit.

Hmm. Why would this one be password-protected?

She tried the password they'd just hacked from Quentin's e-mail account.

wasabi

Nothing.

Crap.

Lola tried the first password from Quentin's browser list.

proustmadeleine

No comment.

No time for comment, even. She was in.

Lola quickly scanned the document titles.

Wait.

Did I just see what I think I saw?

Lola opened one document, then another, to be sure.

Oh. My. God.

This, I'm guessing, is what you call a "break in the case."

Forty-one

Lola had found four large documents in Quentin's Other file. Three were entitled, respectively, *Gay Best Friend*; *So Many Men, So Little Taste*; and *Eenie Meenie Minie Man*.

Mimi's book, Daphne's book, Honey's book.

With Quentin's contact information on the title page, under each of the dead women's names.

Turns out crossword puzzles aren't all Quentin writes.

Lola skimmed each book. There were some differences here and there—where Quentin had written "red lipstick," the published versions said "Cover Girl Scarlettastic"—but it was clear that what Lola was looking at was not a final draft. And—yes—there, indeed, on Quentin's computer, was the scene with the mouse.

My God.

No wonder Quentin can afford to bid on a 1948 Joe DiMaggio whatever. He's a goddamn ghostwriter.

And, given that Quentin was so far the only clear, specific link among the three authors, a possible murderer.

And, given the fact that I set him up with Mimi, I am a possible accessory, but I'm not even going to think about that.

Whoa, whoa, whoa.

Major question.

If Quentin is the killer, why would he ask me to find . . . the killer?

No no, that one's easy, Lola thought. The crossword thing: it's part of his pathology. He dares people to solve his puzzles.

Lola reached for the phone. Doug is not gonna believe— Shit.

I *could* call Doug, Lola reasoned. Tell him I just happened to be noodling around on Quentin's hard drive?

Right after the phone call about the password? The *big fat lie* phone call about the e-mail password, which, given that what I found was in a folder protected by a password I found myself, turned out to be an absolute waste of a betrayal of trust in the first place?

Better not, Lola sighed.

Not like I can call Annabel either.

She went to the kitchen, sliced open a grapefruit, and, feeling very alone, tried to sort this all out.

Let's see. It's common for famous people to have ghostwriters for their memoirs and inspirational/self-help books—but that's because they're not writers. It's also common for companies called book packagers to come up with a concept for, say, a teen novel, and then outsource the writing—but that's not necessarily ghostwriting, even if the author uses a pseudonym, because they're only writing *Dear Mom, Ran off With a Boy Band, Love, Shelley* to pay the rent until they break into the *New Yorker*.

But an actual writer with a secret ghostwriter?

Strange, but not outlandish, Lola mused. She poured some leftover coffee into a glass and plopped in some ice. You could have a concept, a voice, even a hook, but somehow lack the follow-through for a whole book. Hey, it made sense. You get a call from an agent or publisher, if you're one of those people who just gets a call from an agent or publisher. "We think your column/blog/letter would be a great concept for a book," they say. "But if you're not sure writing an entire book is really your speed, *we can help you out.*"

Enter the fixer: Quentin Frye.

But wouldn't Quentin's various publishers know about each other? Lola wondered. Wouldn't they have noticed the three murdered authors' books on his ghostwriting résumé and called the cops?

Not necessarily. A *guy* writing popular chick lit? I'd call that a secret you avoid putting in writing. I'd call Quentin someone who gets work purely on the word of his agent.

Okay, but wouldn't his agent notice the coincidence? Every author he ghostwrites for winds up, much like a ghost, dead?

Not, Lola thought cynically, if sales are *that* good.

Just for the heck of it, Lola woke up the kitchen computer and entered Quentin's name into the WhoRepresents.com agent/client database, snickering as always at the fact that the Web address also spelled WhorePresents.com.

Nothing.

I don't even want to think about the possibility that he gets all this work without an agent. If he is, he's clearly not spending the 15 percent commission he's saving on his wardrobe.

Lola poured sugar syrup into her coffee from a wee pitcher in the fridge—an iced-coffee trick Doug, adorable Doug, had learned from his postcollege espresso-slinging days in Madison. Lola's chest tightened again, but she wrenched her thoughts away from her husband. Her awesome, skilled, thoughtful husband who made sure her iced coffee was always sweet. Her supersmart, devoted husband whose innocence and trust she was currently—

Lola wrenched her thoughts away from her husband on the second try.

Now, about the killer part. Quentin?

I mean, *Quentin?*

It didn't make sense, but right now, what else could?

Write the books, kill the authors, drive up sales, laugh all the way to the royalty bank.

Quentin. My God, Quentin.

Wait, another question. Do ghostwriters get royalties, or just one lump payment? Shoot. I think just lump payments! Then how would this work?

I don't know.

Eye on her prize, Lola determined to forget about the small hole that the royalties question had poked in her theory. She ticked through the murders in her head. She had seen Quentin leaving the party just before Mimi was killed. He'd been released from the cops before Daphne's body was discovered. And he—unlike Wilma, or Reading Guy, who was looking at this point like a pretty shabby stalker—could easily blend in at Bergdorf's. Lola could see the *New York Day* story now.

"Acquaintances were shocked by the news of Frye's deadly double life. 'Quentin always seemed like such a gentle guy. Guess that's exactly how he had us fooled,' said stunned—and stunning—redhead writer Lola Somerville, who, due to her pivotal role in exposing the killer, was awarded a lucrative contract for a book based on the murders."

Book. Murders. Hang on. Lola chugged the last sips of her iced coffee—ever since the Great Keyboard Root Beer Flood of 2004, open beverages were prohibited from her desk—dropped the glass in the sink, and raced back to her office computer.

The fourth book on Quentin's hard drive. How could it have slipped my mind? If Quentin's actually the killer, I've got to warn the author that she's likely his next victim.

The document's title was *Left Behind*. Its author—author?—was Nina Sambuca.

Lola rolled her eyes. Did it *have* to be Nina?

Nina Sambuca had undergone more than one transformation that seemed suspiciously to match market demand. She'd first made a name for herself as the bad-girl author (if she'd even written it!) of the best-selling pharma-memoir *Xanax Planet*. Then, post-rehab, a reformed Sambuca shocked readers with—and sold a kabillion copies of—*Like a Virgin: The New Chastity*, a footnoted screed whose cover featured the leggy author wearing a corset and that garnered rave reviews from the likes of Alexandria Coltish and Camille Paglia. ("This crazy bitch doesn't know what she's talking about," read Paglia's blurb. "Then again, the sexual daemonism of chthonian nature is an apotropaion, a fecund signifier of the omophagy of a world seeking cathexis. I couldn't put it down!")

Then Nina found God. According to Amazon.com, which Lola had quickly searched, *Left Behind*—dubbed "church lit"— was the story of a lonely Christian single whose friends are all married. It had just been published.

Lola looked up Nina's number, which she'd had since the time they'd spoken together on a Women Writers panel at the Y. During the panel, Lola had said, "I have a question for the moderator: how come the Y never has panels called Male Writers?" After the panel, she and Nina had said "Let's definitely have lunch." She and Nina had definitely never had lunch, and Lola had definitely never been invited back to speak at the Y.

As unlikely as it is that Nina will believe me, and as little as I would actually miss her, I'm going to have to alert her to the danger she's in. The world's least threatening-looking killer is on the loose—and she could be next.

Warn her, then figure out how to nab him.

Lola reached for the phone just as it rang.

Ooh, maybe it's Annabel.

"Lola? It's Quentin."

Forty-two

Play it cool, Somerville.

"Hey, Quentin. How ya holding up?"

And by "holding up," Lola added in her mind, I mean "holding up under the guilt of having killed your own girlfriend, and others, for your own profit."

"As well as can be expected, thanks. Thanks for everything, actually—that's why I called."

Thanks for having gotten so far off the trail that I got in another murder?

"Quentin, I really—"

"No, seriously. I know you must have had something to do with their catching Wilma, and wow, am I sleeping better now."

I'll bet.

"Hey look, we just want this all to be over," Lola said. Play dumb. Reveal nothing. He'll never guess you've got his number.

"Hey listen, are you going to Nina Sambuca's reading tonight?"

"Thinking about it," Lola replied quickly. Whoa. Didn't even know she had one. "Are you?"

"Yeah, I feel like it's time to, you know, get back out there," said Quentin. "Not to date—I mean, leave my apartment."

Mmhmm. Smooth. "Sounds like a plan," said Lola. "Remind me where the reading is?"

"Well, it's at Theo's." Natch. The hip downtown church-slash-bar. "But first I'm taking my sister Penny out for drinks. That's what I'm really calling about. I mean, I know readings aren't your favorite."

True.

"So would you like to join us?"

"What's the occasion?"

"Hmmm, you'll find out when you get there," Quentin said coyly.

I am completely grossed out by all this nice-guy, good-brother posing.

"Sure," said Lola. Couldn't hurt. Maybe he'll loosen up over a lager and say something incriminating. "Where and when?"

Lola took a plum from the fridge and ate it over the sink, ignoring the juices that ran down her wrist and into the crook of her elbow. Then, grabbing her garden scissors, she headed outside. The air was humid and sticky, the sky the color of a nickel. Lola hunkered down with her giant potted nasturtium, whose orange-flecked afro needed some serious trimming.

Less than two weeks ago, thought Lola, everything was normal. I was irritated and restless, and fundamentally happy. My bedrocks were in place. I never worried about my marriage, never worried about my best friendship. I never thought about determining when to have children; I just thought I'd know. I never exploited other people's murders for my own professional gain.

I never felt this lonely.

Lola went inside and came back out with the phone. She sat down on her front steps.

"Hi, Mommy."

"Lola! Is anything wrong?"

"No, Mommy, everything's fine."

"Let me check the calendar—is it Mother's Day? No, that was a month ago," Mrs. Somerville said with exaggerated puzzlement. "Then to what do I owe—"

"Can't a girl just call her mom to say hello?" Lola couldn't help laughing.

"You tell me!" Her mother was laughing now, too.

"Sometimes," said Lola, mock serious. "*Sometimes.*"

"How are you holding up, sweetie? I know this can't be an easy time."

"Oh, you know," said Lola. "Eh."

"I know. I'm just so glad you have Doug and Annabel."

Lola swallowed. "Me, too." She switched ears. "Hey, Mom? Listen. There's something I want to tell you."

"Of course, honey."

Lola took a breath. "I really don't know if I'm ready to have kids yet."

"Oh!" said Mrs. Somerville. "Goodness. Let me just sit down."

Jesus. "Mom, I—I'm sorry if it's upsetting," said Lola.

"Are you kidding?" said Mrs. Somerville. "I'm relieved."

"Relieved? You mean, you don't think I'm ready, either?" Lola found herself oddly hurt.

"Oh, no no no. It's just, do you know how many horrific things go through a mother's head when her kid says, 'There's something I want to tell you'?! Let me just take a moment to purge the dooms-day scenarios from my brain. I mean, Lyme disease, some sort of terrible fire, the Peace Corps . . ."

Lola had to laugh again. "Sorry, Mom. But so—you're not, like, disappointed?"

"Disappointed that you don't want to have kids until you're ready? Hardly."

I have really underestimated my mother, thought Lola.

"But just one thing, Lulu," her mother added. "You'll never be ready."

"Wait, what?"

"I mean, not that you'll never be ready. I mean, *one* is never ready. Not truly ready. There's no way you could be until you actually have the kid, and really, not even then. You just kind of decide that you're willing to wing it, is all," said her mother. "You'll know when you're ready to do that."

"I will?"

"Yes, you will. In fact, I remember the very night your father and I—"

"Thanks, Mom," Lola interrupted. "Well, okay. Now I'm the one who's relieved."

"I can understand why you're thinking about it now, Lulu, what with all the death you're in the midst of. Cycle of life thoughts, 'How can I bring a child into this world?' thoughts, that kind of thing."

"You're so right, Mom." Looking around, right at that moment, Lola appreciated the tangled, thriving beauty of her garden more than ever. She ran her hands over the fuzzy leaves of a foxglove.

"But don't worry. This will blow over, and you will definitely know. I trust you to trust yourself."

"Thanks, Mom."

"Okay?"

"Okay."

"So, any plans for tonight?"

"Eh, Doug's going to the movies, I've got a book reading. Nothing major." Oops. Maybe I shouldn't even have mentioned that I'm leaving the house. "But it's right here in Brooklyn, so—" Crap! That was even worse. Now she'll think I'm walking home, right down dark, deserted Murdered Author Boulevard, instead of taking a nice safe cab. Quick, think of a cover—

"Oh, good. I'm so glad you're getting out."

Again with the underestimation.

"Love you, Mom."

"You, too, Lulu."

Okay, thought Lola as she scrambled an egg with some just-snipped chives. So I don't have to plan my whole life right now.

Only the part where I try, once again, to trap a killer.

Or at least keep him from killing again.

She put on her favorite plaid vintage cotton kilt, which had remained on her floor since her day at Coney and, bonus, went rather adorably with Keds—not exactly *running* shoes, but better than clogs—and left a note for Doug. "Out with Quentin & his sis; then, God help me, Nina Sambuca reading at Theo's. Love you."

Fifteen minutes later, Lola boarded the subway. She was halfway to Manhattan before she realized her first mistake.

Forty-three

Did I learn nothing from my sheltered childhood?

Always tell someone where you're going to be.

Lola's note to Doug had mentioned where Nina's reading was, but not where she was meeting Quentin beforehand. No one on the planet knew where she'd be. Maybe not even Penny who, for all Lola knew, had been part of some sort of ruse. So arguably, she was about to wind up alone in a dark bar with a killer. Not even when she was Internet dating had she broken the "always leave word" rule.

Of course, Lola sighed, she'd always told Annabel.

I am going into this utterly, totally, completely without backup.

Lola sank down into the orange plastic subway seat.

Also? I am a melodramatic bonehead. I'll just leave a message for—or hey, even text Doug—when I get aboveground. Further, here's an ego check: tonight's target is Nina, not you.

Lola peeled the backs of her bare thighs off the edge of the seat, sat up straighter, and looked around the car. She remembered, and she could not believe she remembered it wistfully, the idiotic, purely hypothetical subway game that she and Annabel used to play: "If you *had* to sleep with someone on this car, who would it be?" The challenge was, passing was not allowed. On a rough night, the choice would come down to a man in full clown makeup and a woman eating sardines straight out of the can. On a good night, even though this was not the goal, the game would actually net Annabel a date.

For old times' sake, Lola settled on a scruffyish, hangdoggy guy at the end of the car, mainly out of pity; if she were to follow through, she'd just get him home, get him showered, and send him back into the world for women who actually found him to be their type. That wasn't how the game worked, either, but Lola's heart wasn't in it, and Annabel wasn't exactly there to call her on it.

Lola got out of the subway in Manhattan's East Village, which had been exactly as grubby as it was depicted in *Rent*, right around until *Rent* came along. Before, you couldn't walk a block without finding a drug deal, a flophouse, or a transvestite. Now you couldn't walk a block without finding a Fugu-tini, a puggle, or a transvestite. Only now the transvestites were leading the *Rent* bus tours.

Hmm, this place is new. Lola stopped to read the menu outside a restaurant called Foam.

Twice-seared compassionately raised pork belly with wilted infant lettuces, root beer lollipop and rosemary air.

Okay, no.

It's no fun scoffing without Doug, Lola thought, recalling the time he'd taken her to that place called just 4, or 2, or ~, or whatever it was, and when she'd asked the waiter to remind her what was in the ravioli that came with the breast of pheasant, he had replied, "It's a continuation of the pheasant," which immediately caused Doug to snarf his Burgundy.

Which reminds me, Lola thought: gotta call Doug.

But as she got out her phone, still moved by her memory of the subway game, Lola found herself dialing Annabel instead.

"Hi, Bella. I know we're like not talking right now. This is— this is totally stupid. But I'm meeting someone at a bar—meeting Quentin, not a date—and Doug is at a total cell-phone-not-even-on-vibrate movie, and long story short, I just wanted you . . . I just wanted someone to know where I am. Just like, you know, old times. It's stupid, I know, I'm sorry. Okay, bye."

Shit.

Lola, kicking herself, called back. "Jesus. Meant to say. We're going to Yard. Sorry. Bye."

Such. A. Heel.

Lola felt no better, no less alone.

She opened the door to Yard, thinking again about Annabel and the subway game.

Then it hit her. That guy she'd picked was totally Ethan Hawke.

I have to admit I like this place, Lola thought as she opened the door to Yard.

The bar was almost all outdoors, like that Bohemian beer garden in Queens—capital *B* Bohemian, as in the region in the Czech Republic, not as in *alternative*—where Doug had taken her on an early date. But no Czech soccer jerseys or posters for the famed U Fleku beer hung here. Yard's ceiling and walls were practically solid wisteria and grapevines. Emerald tendrils braided themselves with strings of white lights; scattered purple blossoms, just beginning to emerge for the season, hung down like fragrant lanterns.

Lola glanced around. No Quentin yet. She leaned against the end of the bar.

A glint of light outside the bar made her turn her head before she even realized it. A glint, then a square-shaped reflection.

Reading Guy.

Well! It's about time.

Lola watched the door. Reading Guy did not come in. She gave him another minute. Still nothing.

Had he even seen me?

Eh, no matter, Lola thought. He's been demoted from prime suspect back down to New York weirdo. We'll probably just see him at Nina's reading, like normal, before Quentin makes his next move.

Guess that's that, thought Lola, vaguely wondering if she'd brushed her teeth before she left. She rummaged around in her bag for some citrus Altoids, which tasted like Sour Patch Kids for grown-ups, and which Oona had turned her on to during her own battles with first-trimester nausea.

Deep in her bag, Lola's hand brushed against the cellophane window of an envelope. Why do I walk around carrying junk mail? Lola wondered, fishing it out while she peeked over the bar for a trash can.

Oh.

I had completely forgotten.

It was the envelope that Quentin's doorman had asked her to leave in Quentin's apartment.

Lola held it up to the light, which, in the near-dark, was useless.

Let's see. If I get the bartender to make me some tea, or some sort of embarassingly unseasonal Irish coffee, maybe I can find a way to steam it open. Or maybe—oh, fuck it.

Lola tore open the envelope.

Inside was a check for—let's just say, enough for at least one 1948 Joe DiMaggio whatever-you-call-it. It had been issued by a company Lola had never heard of called The Cover. Lola flipped the check over.

Bingo. The check stub, which had been folded behind, contained just the word Lola had forgotten she'd been looking for.

"Royalties."

Laugh all the way to the royalty bank.

Even in the dim light, Lola saw a shadow pass across the check. She looked up.

"Hey, Lola," said Quentin.

Forty-four

Thinking quickly, Lola dropped her entire bag on the floor. As Quentin leaned over to scoop up its contents—how long have I been carrying around that avocado, Lola wondered, and why?—she slipped the check into her pocket.

"Didn't mean to startle you, Lola," Quentin smiled.

Yeah, right. "No worries," said Lola. "Guess we're all a little on edge these days."

For some reason, Lola was expecting Quentin to look different, now that she had a bead on him. But there he was, the same old Quentin she'd once had a soft spot for, even though blonds had never been her type, even though he'd really annoyed her when he'd gone through that brief phase of signing his e-mails "*Namaste*, Quentin." There he was, in his full worn-cork-heeled-sandaled glory, ten-pound book under his skinny arm, what was left of his hair ready for a trim, face probably needing some sunscreen, even at night. It was still, and would never be, the face of a killer. Which was surely why, until now, no one suspected but Lola.

Hmm. Seven-letter word for mild-mannered friend who had

everyone fooled: *Quentin*. *Assassin*. No wait, that has four *S*s. *Butcher?* M-U-R-D-E—

"So you want to grab a table?" Quentin asked.

Did he just catch me staring?

"Penny will be here any sec," he added.

"Sure," said Lola, pointing to his book. "By the way, whatcha reading?" *Murderous Greed for Dummies?*

He held the book out, practically grunting under its weight.

A Heartbreaking Work of Staggering Genius: The Original Unedited Manuscript.

"How is it?" asked Lola. "Long?"

"So far." Quentin nodded.

"Hey, guys!" Penny arrived, still in her scrubs. How did she always look great with no makeup and no sleep?

A hostess in gingham culottes and flip-flops led them toward a side table. How am I going to play this? Lola worried. How am I going to play this without my best wingmen?

By ear, she sighed to herself. By ear.

They ordered a round of flower-themed cocktails—Lola, eyeing Quentin, chose a Bloody Marigold, and then, not knowing what else to say, quizzed Penny about comfortable clogs until the drinks came.

"So!" said Lola. "What's the occasion?" She entertained a brief vision of Quentin putting down his travel-size Purell, pulling a knife, and snarling, "Your death."

As it turned out, the news was almost as bad.

"Penny," Quentin said, raising his Bee Balm Bellini, "has just sold her book."

Christ.

"Cheers!" Lola grinned, clinking her glass all around. Did Penny not ask for my help with the proposal, like, less than two weeks ago? "That's awesome, Penny. Who's the publisher?"

"Jitney. You know, one of those hip downtown ones. They're an imprint of someone, forget who."

"Right," Lola nodded. A nasty thought came to her. A nasty, but probably pretty accurate, thought.

"When on earth are you going to have a chance to write it?"

"Guess I'm just gonna have to make time!" Penny said, shrugging a shoulder coyly.

Mmmhmm. I'll bet Quentin is totally writing her book.

"But listen, Lola," Quentin said, leaning forward. "*shER*"—he made air quotes around the title—"is a complete secret right now. No one but her publisher knows. We just wanted to tell you," he added, looking over at Penny, "because we both sort of—well, we consider you an inspiration."

Just for a moment, Lola's evening sucked a little less.

"Yeah, we do," Penny said. "But just please don't say anything until the deal is inked, signed, sealed, delivered, the whole nine. I just—I'm a scaredy-cat, except when it comes to blood. I just don't want to jinx anything."

I do! thought Lola. "Of course," she replied, turning an invisible key on her lips and tossing it over her shoulder.

Quentin, meanwhile, was reaching for his cell. "Excuse me one sec," he said, holding the phone up to one ear and sticking a finger in the other.

"Anyway . . ." Lola smiled, hating them both.

"Anyway!" said perky Penny.

"No *way*!" said Quentin, suddenly paler than ever. "Not *Nina*!"

Forty-five

Lola and Penny stared.

I'm wrong about the killer again?

Nina's dead?

These were Lola's thoughts, not necessarily in order of importance.

"Oh, come on," Quentin was saying. "You couldn't possibly—I haven't read *Karenina* since like sixth grade."

Wait, what?

"*Ivan Ilych*, yeah, but—" Quentin paused to listen again. "Well, look, must be that someone just got careless. You know how many people—" Realizing Lola and Penny were listening, he remembered his manners. "Hang on one sec," he told the caller, then covered the phone's mouthpiece.

"Nina. Her book. Some blog revealed that portions of it appear to have been cribbed from *Anna Karenina*," he said. "Bit of an uproar. The publisher recalled it. There's no reading tonight."

Lola's head spun. Could Quentin have done that, purloined from Tolstoy? He seemed way, way too smart for that. But then

who did, and *why*? And could no editor have noticed at some point during the process that there are not that many horses named Frou-Frou in New York? Little dogs in bags, maybe, but not horses? Could Quentin have just scrapped any plans to kill Nina, considering that her book may be dead in the water? Or will whatever copies do sell become some major pre-recall collectors' item, like the Jennifer Aniston doll? *Now* will people realize that Nina Sambuca is a big fake?

"How on earth could that have happened?" Lola asked.

Quentin shrugged and shook his head. "Honestly, beats the heck out of me." His tone was light, but Lola could have sworn she saw something dark behind his eyes that she'd never seen before.

"Well, don't worry," Penny said. "I promise not to crib anything from *Coma*."

"Hey, isn't that Annabel's friend?" Quentin, perhaps eager to change the subject, had spotted Leo through the crowd at the bar.

Lola started at the mention of Annabel's name. She turned her head. Leo was solo. Crap/whew.

Quentin's wave caught Leo's eye. He smiled and walked over.

Wait. I told Annabel I'd be here. How does Leo fit in? Has she told him what's going on between us? How would she have explained the part about how *he* is basically what's going on between us?

"Quentin, Lola . . . Doctor," said Leo, clad in his mandals and a nice striped shirt Doug would dismiss as "Banana Republican." Lola always thought it was so gentlemanly, the way Leo greeted everyone individually. But a little less gentlemanly, perhaps, the way his eyes seemed to rest a little longer on Penny.

Dammit, Annabel, I'm not gonna say anything, but if, *if*, you wake up and realize you want this guy, you've got to act faster. The man is not made of wood.

Quentin introduced Penny and Leo. The waitress swung by to take Leo's order. "Rest of you okay?" she asked. Quentin and Lola

declined another round, but Penny accepted, draining her first Ginkgo and Tonic as the waitress walked away. "I love it when I'm not on call," she said, excusing herself to go to the bathroom.

"May I?" Leo gestured toward a chair. "Just waiting for Annabel. Could be a while," he added with a rueful smile. "So what's new? How are your drinks? Where's Doug?"

"Hey, she's allowed out without her husband," said Quentin.

"Only on Saturdays," Lola joked, though actually feeling a little defensive. "So listen to what just happened."

She started telling Leo the Nina story, which somehow morphed into a conversation between the two men about Russian futurism.

A really *long* conversation about Russian futurism.

During which, thankfully, the waitress arrived with Penny's drink. "Sorry for the delay," she said, nodding her head back toward the bar. "We're slammed."

"No problem," said Quentin. "Where's Penny?"

Lola could not volunteer fast enough to check on her.

"Penny?" Lola pushed open the door to the bathroom, which was lit only with a—what was that smell?—gardenia-scented candle. No answer. A woman in a backless top and a cowboy hat tossed her paper towel in a basket and squeezed past Lola on her way out.

Lola was alone.

"Penny? It's Lola." The two stalls were large. One door was open, the other closed. She peeked under. Too dark to see feet.

"Penny?"

Nothing.

Lola fished in her bag. She turned on her fancy cell phone and held it under the door. There in the bluish shadows lay two scrub-green legs ending in two maroon Dansko clogs.

Forty-six

Oh, God. Oh, God, Penny.

Trembling, still on her hands and knees, Lola called 911.

Okay. Okay. Think. Think. What else? She got to her feet and grabbed the doorknob. Ah. She turned the tab to lock it, then patted her hands along the wall. Double ah. A light switch.

Click.

Suddenly the bathroom didn't look so romantic. On hands and knees again, Lola peeked back under the door. She still couldn't see much, and she couldn't climb through from the other stall without hitting Penny. There seemed to be no blood, no bruises, no nothing. Yet as far as she could tell, Penny was not breathing.

Oh, no. Oh no no no no no.

Shaking so hard her bangles clattered, Lola stumbled to her feet and fled the bathroom. She flagged the nearest waitress, explaining why she might want to keep more people from going in. Then she turned toward the table, heart hammering, thoughts churning.

Quentin, there's something I need to tell you.

Looks like you're not the killer.

While I'm on the subject, Lola thought, neither is Wilma, given that she's apparently still in custody.

Guess Reading Guy's been promoted once again. Though I could swear I never saw him come in here.

Then again, Somerville, that's what killers do. Fail to be seen. I should have been watching.

I should have been watching.

"Quentin," Lola said. "There's something I have to tell you." Just then the EMTs burst through the front door. The hostess pointed toward the back. The stretcher left a trail of shocked, gasping patrons in its wake.

"Quentin," Lola said, loudly, to get his attention back. She nodded her head back toward the restroom, where the EMTs were converging. "It's Penny." Quentin made a small sound and flew off his chair, knocking it over.

Lola polished off her drink in one gulp, then Quentin's, then Penny's. She reached for Penny's first glass, too, but Penny had drained it dry, leaving only a few black seeds on the bottom.

Leo, sad-eyed and ever solicitous, held out his glass.

Lola, reeling a little, put up a hand. "I'm good."

There was commotion behind them. Far as Lola could see, the EMTs were wheeling Penny out a back door. She saw Quentin's beanpole figure trailing behind. This was not a time to interrupt. She'd just have to call him.

Lola turned to Leo, helpless.

"Leo, I can't—I—what am I supposed to even say at this point?"

"How about 'yes' to a ride home?"

"Yes to a ride home," said Lola.

Leo dropped a few twenties on the table while Lola stood uncertainly, dazed. "I mean, after we talk to the cops," she added. She nodded toward the entrance, where two had just come in. Why not Bobbsey? she wondered, then remembered that with

Penny's book deal still a secret, there was no real reason for him to be there. Him or Wally, for that matter.

Wow, am I on the cutting edge this time, she thought, without joy.

When the police had finished with their questions, Leo gestured toward the exit.

"Wait," Lola asked. "What about Annabel?"

"Oh. Yeah. She texted me while you were in the bathroom," Leo said. "She bailed."

"Ah," said Lola.

Now I feel double-sick. She probably canceled when she realized I'd be there, too.

As she followed Leo out of the bar, steps heavy, she let her gaze rest on some dangling wisteria: so lovely—so incongruously so.

You know what? she thought. That's it. I'm done. Done with all the mediocre sleuthing that's coming between me and my loved ones, including my suffering garden. Quentin's got more on his mind than Mimi right now. Wilma's effectively in the clear. Bobbsey knows what he's doing. That's it. I'm going home to wait up for my husband and salvage my best friendship—along with, first thing tomorrow, my poppies. A book idea will come, but not like this.

I quit.

No lie this time.

I quit.

Lola got into Leo's SUV. She closed the door on the summer drizzle, closed the door on her role as crappy detective. Leo put on a Buena Vista Social Club CD, and they rode for a good while without speaking, Lola relaxing a bit into her hollow relief.

"So what are you working on these days?" Leo said as they rumbled past Brooklyn's Prospect Park and, on a prime corner across the street, the columned, zinnia-circled home that she knew to be Jennifer Connelly's. Doug, citing the cinematic importance of *The Rocketeer*, had pointed it out. And walked by it whenever possible.

"You know, the usual," said Lola. "Same articles, new headlines."

"Any new books in mind?" he asked.

"Not without any new ideas," she said.

"Well, don't they say you gotta write what you know?" Leo asked. It was possibly the least helpful thing he'd ever said, thought Lola. "Like with Penny and her ER memoir. Looks like maybe that deal's off now, though." He shook his head.

Lola started to look at Leo, then caught herself and stopped.

There was no way Leo could have known about Penny's book deal.

Forty-seven

"Looks like," Lola said, fake offhand, her mind racing.

How does he know, how does he know, how does he know?

What does this mean, what does this mean, what does this mean?

Lola's thoughts spun first back to the last time she'd been in Leo's car, that time after Oona's shower, though they'd never actually gone anywhere. Now that she thought about it, the spa Leo said he'd been working on was right next door to Penny's publisher.

"So did you do any work at Jitney Books?" Lola asked on a hunch.

"Yeah," said Leo, eyes on the road. "I created a Tide-Pool Experience."

"Do they mind that you work for the competition?" Lola asked. Her hunch confirmed, she'd moved ahead with a massive bluff.

Which worked. "If they did, I'd be out of business," Leo said. "Once Poncho Books had their whole prairie grass installation—to go with all their prairie skirts, the five minutes they were in style—all the other hip publishers had to have something like it, too." His tone was light, but he'd glanced sharply at Lola as he spoke.

Lola forced a laugh. "Figures."

So. So so so. Lola could practically feel the gears cranking in her head like the inside of an old watch. Leo could have over-heard something about Penny's book while working at Jitney. That's innocent enough. He could also have put in a good word for Annabel at Poncho in some way. Maybe he brought her blog to their attention or even influenced their decision to offer her a contract.

But her earlier hunch was starting, slowly, to take a more sinister shape. She changed the subject, still not entirely sure what she was fishing for.

"So weird and creepy about Penny. I mean, I saw her. No blood, no marks, no nothing. Think maybe some new bartender forgot everything he'd been taught about hemlock?"

Leo raised his eyebrows. Lola, shifting her legs nervously, kicked something beneath her feet. She peeked down just as they passed a round-the-clock construction project: a five-acre Whole Farms Market was going up, complete with an on-site trout hatchery that had rerouted Brooklyn's only natural spring. The bright spotlights briefly illuminated the inside of the car, including what Lola then saw on the floor.

Bulbs. Narcissus. Lola was sure of it.

Which, she was also positive, was poisonous. Like hemlock.

And like wisteria seeds, which, now that she thought about it, were the seeds that she'd seen in the bottom of Penny's glass. Not ginkgo. Wisteria. Poisonous wisteria.

Couldn't the seeds have just fallen in? In theory, yes, but probably not this early in the season—the blooms, after all, were just starting—and how would they have escaped their pods by them-selves?

In other words, Lola determined, I should probably start think-ing about how to get out of this car.

Act casual, Somerville. Real casual. It's Casual Day. It's Casual

City, and you're the mayor. Lola hummed along with the CD while her mind snapped together the remaining puzzle pieces.

The deaths started right after Annabel got her book deal—that is, right after Leo found out about Annabel's book deal. Leo is clearly crazy about Annabel. But exactly how crazy? He probably helped her score the deal in the first place and wanted to help make it a success . . . Could he have been trying to kill off her competition?

He could have popped those seeds into Penny's drink when we were all saying no to a second round. He could have had them on him, or at least known to pop them out of a hanging pod; this could easily look like a terrible accident. He could have blended right into Bergdorf's and could, somehow, have attacked Honey. He could have gotten to the party and killed Mimi before we all met afterward; he *said* he got stuck on the subway like everyone else, but since when does Leo take the subway? He could have—

"Thanks for telling me when Daphne's flight was coming in," said Leo. He was pulling up on the bridge over the Lundy Canal. Speaking of Daphne.

Lola's mind stumbled backward. Of course. Her gut clenched with guilt. She'd been on speakerphone with Annabel, discussing the Daphne return that never was, when Leo had walked in.

Leo stopped the van. The bridge, as always, was dark and deserted. He looked at Lola, all of a sudden distinctly less handsome. Right now, his longish hair made him look less hot, more crazy. His huge, lash-fringed eyes were sunk in soulless shadow. "Let's take a walk," he said.

"Is gas that expensive?" Lola asked. Must stay in van. My one hope for safety is this: Leo will seriously not want to get blood in his precious Escarole.

Something glinted in the muddy moonlight. Leo was holding a small—but sharp enough—root digger.

Or maybe he could deal with a little blood.

"It's not as theme as my other weapons, but it'll have to do," Leo said.

So much for my plan to lunge for the keys and gas pedal, which was probably not airtight to begin with, thought Lola. And I doubt I could outrun him. She reached for her bag, taking all the time she could, and then stepped out into the night.

Forty-eight

This, Lola knew, was the part where the hero stalls for time.

The hero, or the victim.

"Sure could have used that gizmo when I dug—" she cleared her throat, hoping to hide the shaking in her voice "—dug those dandelions this spring," she said. By then, Leo had come around the front of the car to face her.

"Are you serious? You don't have one of these? They're incredibly useful," Leo said. "Please tell me you at least have a spading fork."

"That, yeah," said Lola. "So when did I figure you out?"

"When you saw the obviously-not-ginkgo seeds in Penny's glass."

Hmm. Untrue, but flattering.

"But then why would I get in the car with you?"

"'Cause you're a little reckless and a little desperate for attention and to be where the action is, so you figured you'd make a plan on the fly?"

Hmm. True, but unflattering.

Lola glanced around. The pointy root digger hung from Leo's

hand. The grimy canal yawned at her side. One ratty sneaker, inexplicably, hung by its laces from the single faraway streetlight. A white plastic Key Food bag, borne by a hot, twitchy breeze, dipped and twirled in the air, slapped against the bridge, and then sailed away into darkness.

Time. Need time.

"So Mimi, I get. Daphne, what, you just happened to swing by the airport and offer her a ride?"

Leo nodded. "Not bad."

"Okay, Honey Porter, then. That one's trickier," Lola said. "Gimme a sec."

She pretended to think for a moment, even though she'd already worked most of this one out. "You did the new installation, whatever you call it, in the Bergdorf's salon, didn't you?"

"The Cliffs of Biarritz? Yes, ma'am," said Leo, with some pride. "Tip: if you need to import gorse bushes, go straight to the Basque."

"So what sort of mickey did you slip into her hair product?"

"Warm," said Leo, leaning against his car hood.

"Had to have been something toxic to the touch, or—"

"Warmer," said Leo.

"Or . . . *Fumes.* Toxic fumes. *Poison ivy* fumes." Lola knew that her father would break into hives if he so much as breathed anywhere near the offending plant. "You mad-scientisted the oil off the plant, slipped it into her kerastase extra-volume serum blah-blah whatever, so that when she sat under the dryer, she was overcome."

"Hot, hot, hot," said Leo. "But you missed one. Or, rather, *I* missed one. And you helped."

"What?"

"Blanca."

"I'm not following," Lola said.

"I know you're not," Leo said with a sneer. "Remember that day when you saw me on Atlantic Avenue and I slowed down but didn't stop?"

"Yeah," Lola said. "You were with Annabel—oh, wait." A tiny

bubble of joy swelled somewhere inside her. *Yes.* Annabel was blow-ing her off most of the time, but not that one. "No, you weren't with Annabel. You ran into Blanca outside Starbooks, thought you'd take advantage of the opportunity to try to get rid of her, but then you saw me and thought I'd seen her, so it was too risky."

"Again, very hot," said Leo.

Poor Blanca, Lola thought. She'd rather die than be consid-ered a chick lit author, and she almost did both.

"And that brings us to Penny," she said.

"Yeah, with that one *I* got a little careless," Leo admitted. "Heard about her new deal today while I was over at Jitney, got annoyed—I mean, it's like, everyone and his sister has a book deal, you know?"

Yes, I do know.

"So, not my best work, but crime of passion, what are ya gonna do?" Leo said.

"And the others weren't? Crimes of passion?"

Leo smiled, teeth as shiny as his car. He held up his hands, one still holding the pointy item that was still holding Lola's primary interest. "Guilty," he said jauntily, then waxed serious. "That's how much I love her."

"Sweet," nodded Lola.

"I turned the honcho at Poncho onto Annabel's blog—then I just had to get the competition out of the way," he said. "I know they get a brief blip with the murdered authors publicity and all, but in the long run, it's better. Thought maybe I'd even scare other would-be chick lit writers into tearing up their proposals."

He took a step toward Lola. "Didn't think I'd have to take *you* out, though," he said. "I mean, it's not like your book is much competition." He took another step toward Lola. "And women think I'm 'unthreatening.' " He smirked.

Leo raised his weapon.

Forty-nine

Doug, appearing behind Leo in the nick of time, grabbed his right arm just as Annabel grabbed his left. Surprise on their side, they wrestled Leo to the bridge. Lola heard a click.

Doug's collectible Batcuffs.

Leo, hands chained to a girder behind him, looked at Annabel with pained, penitent longing. He was defeated in his murderous rampage but, evidently, not in his obsession.

Doug turned back to Lola, who threw herself on her husband. "Doug!" she cried. "Those cuffs were mint in box!"

Doug grinned and kissed his wife, her cheeks in his hands. "Yeah, but think how much more they're worth now that I can say 'used to apprehend actual villain.'"

Annabel, her back to Leo, joined the group hug, then stepped back. "Yeah, so we got your e-mail."

Lola looked up at Doug with exaggerated embarrassment. "Thanks for the phone," she whispered. Just as she had gotten out of Leo's SUV, she had used the once-reviled gadget to snap a photo of the Escarole, its location, and its weapon-bearing driver. When she'd referred to the dandelions she'd "dug," she was actually using the phone's voice command capability to e-mail the photo to Doug.

"Turns out you *would* use the photo function if your life depended on it," he said.

Lola laughed, then glanced over at Leo. "By the way, do you want to borrow it to call the police?"

"Done," said Annabel. "Now we wait." She pulled a can of Red Bull out of her backpack and offered it around.

"No thanks, still wired from the attempted murder," said Lola. She untangled herself from Doug and looked at them both. "This is a little awkward, considering you guys both hate me."

"Hate's a strong word," said Doug. "I'd say more like . . . love."

Lola melted, a little. She was still puzzled. "But what about all the skulking around and blowing you off and, well, blatant lying that I was off the case?"

"You're a good liar," nodded Doug. "Just not a great one. I knew you were still CSIing. But what was I supposed to do, *make* you stop? Didn't we say something about in sickness and in health, in safety and in reckless, ego-driven danger?"

Lola sighed, tears welling.

"The only part that really upset me was that even after we'd talked about it, you still thought you couldn't be straight with me," said Doug. "No more of that, okay, monkey?"

Lola nodded, chastened. "I am both deeply moved and deeply embarrassed."

"See what we could have had?" It was Leo, hollering out from the bridge. "Just know this was all for you, Annabel."

Annabel turned on the heel of her sneaker to face him. "Next time try just admitting your feelings or asking me on an actual date," she said evenly.

"You mean you would have gone out with me?" he asked.

"No," she said. "But it does seem like a better idea in principle." Leo seemed to think about this.

"Listen, Bella," Lola said. Annabel turned back, braids swinging.

"Just for the record, I get your point. Not every 'great guy' is auto-matic boyfriend material. I'm sorry."

"Well, not every great guy is a martini murderer, either," said Annabel. "But listen, that's not all I wanted to hash out with you."

Just then, the sound of sirens cut through the heavy air; red and blue lights smudged the sky. Two police cars skidded to a stop on the bridge, the Wally Seaport–mobile close behind.

Doug handed the Batcuff key to the cops—"I'm gonna need those back," he added—while Lola accosted Wally. She was gen-uinely surprised to see him, assuming he would have sniffed out the book angle on the Penny story by now. Shouldn't he be home working on *Royalty* now, or back at the *Day*, banging out a piece that would inevitably be entitled "Doc Lit: Dead on Arrival"?

"Why aren't you covering the murder?" she asked.

Wally, for his part, was not surprised to see Lola. "What mur-der?" he asked.

Fifty

Lola's phone rang. When she turned toward her bag, Wally took the opportunity to duck away and pester the cops.

"Lola, it's Quentin."

"Oh my God, Quentin."

"Save your condolences, Somerville!" Lola had never heard Quentin sound so giddy. "I'm with her at the hospital right now. Penny's gonna be fine."

"Oh, my God. Oh, thank God," said Lola. "You guys, Penny's okay!" she yelled to Doug and Annabel, who scurried over to eavesdrop.

"Quentin, what on earth happened?"

"Strangest thing. Wisteria poisoning. The restaurant insists they check the vines for seed pods daily to avoid exactly that. I guess the cops are still poking around. And—"

Before Lola could tell him about the cops poking around right next to her in Leo's van, he interrupted himself.

"Oh! Lo, there goes the toxicologist I've been trying to talk to. Apparently she's been distracted; some starlet got bitten by her own illegal kinkajou. Lemme go grab the doctor—"

"Okay," Lola jumped in quickly, "can you just pass the phone to Penny, if she's up for talking?"

"Sure. Here ya go—!" Quentin was off and running.

"Hello?" Penny's voice sounded weak, but Lola was glad to hear it, even if this did mean her book would be coming out after all.

"Penny, I'm so glad you're okay!" said Lola.

"You and me both," she said. Lola figured she'd hold off, for now, on telling her that there was one person who wasn't so glad. She glanced over at Leo, who by then was staring soulfully at Annabel from the back of a squad car.

"Say, Penny, I don't want to keep you, but can I ask you a question in confidence?"

"Of course," said Penny. "I mean, Lola, I might be dead if you hadn't found me when you did. I shall deny you nothing."

Lola laughed uncomfortably. "I'll cut to the chase. How did Quentin get into ghostwriting?" Doug looked puzzled. Annabel didn't.

"Wait, how did you—" Penny started.

"Doesn't matter. I know it's a secret."

"Okay—" Penny paused, then went on. "Guess it couldn't hurt to tell you this part. There was this patient a couple years ago, I guess she thought I played some major role in saving her kid's life— scooter accident, I think it was—and so she was like, 'Is there anything I can do to repay you?' And I was like, 'Well, I'm sick of loaning money to my brother.' I told her Quentin wrote crosswords for a living, and she was like, 'Well, can he write more than one word at a time?' And I said, 'Yeah, I think so. His first job after graduation was a staff writer for *Corduroy Aficionado*. And the lady goes, 'Give me his e-mail; I'll take care of him.' And that was that."

Aha. Patient zero. Which also perhaps explains why Quentin doesn't seem to have an agent. It all began with this person, whoever she was. "I don't suppose you can tell me who that patient was," Lola said.

"Honestly, I don't even remember her name," said Penny. "I

didn't think much of it at the time. If it were someone famous or something, I'd be like, 'Well, I can't violate HIPAA regulations by telling you it was Fane Jonda.'" She lowered her voice. "Anyway, here comes Quentin."

"Thanks, Penny. That was helpful. Keep feeling well, okay?"

"What was that all about?" Doug asked.

"Tell ya on the way home."

By then the police were ready to speak with Lola. A blond woman in a sharp Dana Scully suit handed Doug his Batcuffs, flashed a badge, and introduced herself to Lola.

"Out of curiosity, where's Detective Bobbsey?" Lola asked.

"In the hospital," came the answer.

"Oh, no!"

"His wife just had a baby," came the clarification.

"Oh, yay!" said Lola. She described everything she could to the detective, hoping—actually, believing—that it was the last such statement she'd make for a long, long time. Then she, Doug, and Annabel watched as all the cars pulled away, Leo mouthing the words "Ciao, Bella," from his window.

"This may be inappropriate in some way, but all I want to do right now is go home and eat salt-and-peppered popcorn and watch *Evil Dead*," said Lola. "Who's with me?"

Doug and Annabel raised their hands. They started back over the bridge. Lola noticed for the first time that tonight the canal smelled weirdly of maple syrup. A few stars shone wanly like faraway flashlights in need of new batteries. Lola reached out and held Doug's hand. The sticky night made their palms a little clammy, but neither of them cared.

I guess Annabel's my friend again now, thought Lola, feeling a bit like a third grader. If I keep talking about something else, maybe she'll forget she ever wasn't. Lola opened her mouth.

"So, Lola," said Annabel.

Crap.

Fifty-one

"I think what I have to say to you might also shed some light for Doug on the conversation you just had with Quentin."

Lola blinked. "I'm all ears."

"Listen, I *was* mad at you for the whole anyone-on-her-happily-married-high-horse-could-see-that-you-should-be-dating-Leo thing, I really was."

"As well you should have been."

"But that wasn't all."

Oh, God. What else was she mad about?

Annabel looked behind her. "You guys have to swear not to tell anyone I told you this," she said.

What on earth?

"Awesome!" grinned Doug.

"Look, there's this company," said Annabel, lowering her voice. "They stay under the radar, but they're behind almost all of these books, these trendy, write-by-numbers jobs. They find people with good gimmicks or platforms or whatever, then they develop the concepts, then farm the books out to different writers and publishers. More than one writer per book, sometimes. Writers like Quentin."

This kind of thing didn't sound so secret to Lola. "Well, yeah. Like a book packager?"

"Wait, back up. I thought Quentin wrote puzzles," said Doug.

"Oh yeah," said Lola. "During that time I 'quit' the case, I figured out he'd also ghostwritten Mimi's, Daphne's, and Honey's books."

"So that puzzle you solved," Doug said proudly, adding, "Hey, with *my* fancy flash drive, right? We are a genius."

Lola squeezed Doug's hand and turned back to Annabel. "Right, so a book packager."

Annabel nodded. "Except evil," she said. "Publishers work with this outfit all the time because they're so efficient, but they have no idea how shady the operation is. Seriously. For example: Honey's triplets?"

Lola shuddered.

Annabel leaned in close. "Not. Hers."

"*Really!?*"

"They're her *neighbors'*," Annabel pronounced. "Honey was their *nanny*. This company arranged the whole thing. It's research for her next book, would you believe? They saw a niche for a single-mom-with-triplets title, wanted to fill it."

"Well, that's a relief-slash-totally vile," said Lola.

"I'm telling you. They're responsible for so much more than you think. Except *The Da Vinci Code*," said Annabel. "They're still bummed about that."

Lola knew where this was all going. "And . . . they're doing your book," she said.

Annabel thinned her lips. "Yeah."

"Which is how you know all this?"

"Partly," Annabel said. "Guy who took me to lunch at Qwerty? Well, let's just say it was a . . . long lunch. The second half of which was at his forty million square foot loft. You know. *Ve haf vays.*"

Lola thought for a second. "So this is the other reason you were avoiding me? You didn't want to admit that you'd sold out?

I mean—" Lola corrected herself. "Sorry. You didn't want me to think you had sold out."

"Well . . . yeah. Actually it's the reason I asked for your help at first with the proposal. They actually told me they didn't need me to write one at all—that I should just sit tight and they'd take care of it. You know, have someone experienced, in-house, crank out exactly the concept they needed to develop," Annabel said. "And I thought, that's, like, *wrong*. I wanted to write it for real, to be legit, you know? So I flirted with this guy and made him meet me for lunch so I could give him my own proposal. Which I couldn't have written without your help. And which, naturally, he left on the table." Annabel shrugged helplessly. "So. I tried."

"Are you still gonna work with them?" Doug asked.

"If you call it work. I need the money. If I ever see it," said Annabel. "Far as I know, they don't actually kill people—though they don't exactly step up when their 'authors' die. But mainly, Lo? I was embarrassed. I knew you would think the whole thing was sketchy. I knew you'd be pissed off that you were actually writing—or trying to write—while people sped past you and hit the jackpot, seemingly, or actually, without doing anything. And I knew I might be one of those people. I took everything out on you, like a huge spaz, because I didn't know how to tell you."

"Well, you're right," said Lola. "It is sketchy, and I would have been pissed. But I'd be lying if I said I wouldn't have done the exact same thing in your shoes." In fact, she was smarting a little that this company had never contacted her about a project. Even just to give her the opportunity to say no. Which is what she'd like to think she would have said, but she wasn't entirely sure.

They were just about home. Lola's trumpet vines stirred a bit in the feeble breeze. "Hey, Annabel," said Lola. "By any chance is this company called The Cover?"

"Shh!" said Annabel, eyes wide. "How did you know?"

Just then, a chunky figure emerged from behind a hollyhock.

"Reading Guy!" said Lola.

Fifty-two

"Reading Guy, huh?" said Reading Guy, his hands up. "I expected worse." He pushed up his glasses with one hand, then returned to I-come-in-peace position. "Name's Bailey."

"Any particular reason you're hanging around my wife's garden, Mr. Bailey?" Doug asked.

"The tomatoes aren't even ready yet," said Lola, glaring, hands on hips.

"There's something you need to know about me," Reading Guy said, letting his hands fall by his high-waisted sides. Now his voice sounded remarkably . . . normal. No heavy, snotty breathing, no mention of having crafted any sort of Lola doll using her real fingernail clippings. "Or rather, about your mom."

"My mom?!"

Reading Guy sighed, his froggy head coming to rest even closer to his shoulders. "She hired me."

"Hired you? For what?"

"Well, you know, she worries about you," said Reading Guy, hiking up his pants. "She wanted me to keep an eye on you."

Lola stared.

"I'm a part-time private detective. And a chick lit fan, as you know. Perfect match, she thought."

"You're kidding." Lola squinted, urging her memory to make sense of this. "So that time outside Earl's, why did you tell me I was next?"

"You were. If the killer were going by the *Day* bestseller list. Your mom actually alerted me to that."

Damn, she's good. Lola couldn't help a slight smile. "But what about tonight? If you're supposed to be keeping an eye on me, how come you're here instead of the crime scene? You do know about that, right?"

"Yeah," Reading Guy looked back over Lola's shoulder. "Got there right about when these two did. Managed to lay low." He fiddled with a leaf. "As I said, I'm only part-time. And frankly, not that good. Plus, I don't have a car. Oh, and Bailey's my first name—"

"Why did you bother following me to Coney Island?" she asked. "I was clearly just on a date with my husband, who, not that we're not both feminists, is perfectly capable of protecting me as the situation warrants."

"Oh, I didn't follow you that day," Reading Guy said. He rubbed his glasses on a loose plaid shirttail. "I just had some time to kill before a meeting with the antidevelopment coalition. It's a crime what those voracious capitalists want to do to a place of such deep cultural and historical significance, not to mention un-surpassed corn dogs."

Not only is Reading Guy exactly right about Coney, he's also just kind of a dweeb, Lola realized, contrite. Well, a *huge* dweeb, really, but just a dweeb.

There was just one more stone to turn here.

"Can you hold on for one sec?" Lola asked, stepping aside.

"Dude, who has the better corn dogs, Pete's Clam Stop or Nathan's?" Doug asked Reading Guy.

"Hey, don't forget that other place next to the haunted wax museum," Annabel chimed in.

Lola had gotten out her now-famous phone. "Mom?"

"Lulu, I was just about to call you! I just read they caught the Chick Lit Killer! I can't tell you how relieved I am."

"The article you saw, did it happen to mention me?"

"No, it was just one of those breaking headlines from the *Times*. I get them e-mailed. No full story yet. But why do I have a feeling you had something to do with it?"

Lola laughed.

"No, really. Ask me why."

"What? Oh. Okay, why? Why do you have a feeling I had something to do with it?"

"Because, well, I'd like to think *I* had something to do with your having something to do with it," her mother replied.

"Wait, what?" asked Lola.

"So you did? Have something to do with it?"

"Well, I did kind of catch the killer," said Lola. "Shortly after he caught me."

"Oh honey! I'm so proud! Wait till I tell your father," said Mrs. Somerville. "But first, let me stop talking in circles."

"Yes, please!"

"Lola, about Wilma. I was actually on the phone with her the entire time she was at Bergdorf's. That's how I knew she didn't do it. Had she been charged with the crime, I certainly would have come forward right away. But I called you and gave you a hint when the opportunity arose because I wanted to give you the chance to get ahead of the cops on the case."

Whoa. "Which you knew I was working on because of the guy you hired to keep an eye on me."

Mrs. Somerville paused. "Well, partly because I know *you*. But . . . yes. Also because, well, I found Bailey on The Craig List, and—" said Mrs. Somerville.

"Mom! That's just—it's *embarrassing*. I'm a grown, married woman. You have to figure out how to trust me."

"Lola, I know. I do trust you. Completely. I *admire* you. You're principled, thoughtful, you've got a real head on your shoulders— I couldn't ask for a more wonderful daughter," Mrs. Somerville said.

Lola's heart took an extra beat, sort of the way it used to when a cute boy called. I so needed to hear that, she thought.

"And are you forgetting the part where I threw you a bone?"

"Yes," said Lola, chastised.

"I know you love a caper. I know you're looking for your next big thing," her mother said. "I wasn't at all surprised when Bailey told me he thought you were also trying to find the killer. Though I thought it was pretty funny that for a little while there you seemed to think he was the killer."

Heh. Right.

"But, as you know, *I'm* a little cuckoo," Mrs. Somerville went on. "I trust you—I just don't trust myself not to go crazy with worry, especially when there's a chick lit killer on the loose, even though your book isn't technically chick lit," she said. "Hiring Bailey was an indulgence. For me. I know it was probably a little over-the-top, but you have to admit, so were the circumstances. Anyway, I'm sorry. And I guess we won't be needing him anymore, will we?"

Lola smiled. "Naw, Mom, you can keep him on the payroll if it makes that much difference to you."

"Really?"

"Kidding!" said Lola. "But I understand, Mommy. And, well, it makes me happy to know I make you happy."

"You do, Lulu, you do. Indescribably. Of course, we'd be even happier if you lived closer to home—"

"My next 3.5 million, I'll buy you a pied-à-terre in New York," said Lola. "Want to talk to your gumshoe?"

Lola handed the phone to Reading Guy with a kind smile. "You're fired."

"You guys ready?"

Annabel sat in the TV room flipping channels as Lola peppered the popcorn in the giant wedding-present bowl they loved to hate. On the inside bottom, two smiling turtles in bride and groom gear held hands underneath a pink heart with Lola and Doug's wedding date. Doug always threatened to sell it on eBay, date and all, but kept forgetting, mainly because it was perfect for popcorn, as long as one positioned any burned kernels over the offending reptiles.

"Almost!" Lola called.

Doug grabbed three Lundy Lagers. He and Lola joined Annabel on the couch. They clinked bottles. Lola settled in, her hand in Doug's, her head on Annabel's shoulder. Cheers, indeed.

The next morning, Doug brought Lola coffee in bed.

"What's the occasion?" she asked.

"I love it when you don't get killed."

"I don't get killed pretty much every day," said Lola, pulling him down next to her, wrapping the sheet around them both, and kissing her husband hard. "Tomorrow, if you don't mind, I'll also take a scone."

Fifty-three

Lola watered her garden, giving a silent but impassioned "I still love you" speech to each and every plant. Even you, wisteria.

And after a long shower, in which she employed every scented shampoo, gel, scrub, and wash she'd ever been given by last-minute birthday present shoppers, Lola toasted a bagel, wrapped a towel around her head, and sat down at her computer. Time to buckle down and start that book proposal. Doug, already at his desk, turned around.

"You smell like a smoothie."

Lola grinned, sniffed her arm, nodded in agreement, and—just quick, before she started writing—glanced down the subject lines of her e-mail. "Asbestos turncoat," "wardrobe froth effluvium," "minesweeper bluefish," "Welcome, Quetzalcoatl!" Junk, junk, junk, ju—oops, wait.

"Quetzalcoatl Everett Bloom arrived yesterday, healthy and happy. Mom Oona and Dad Mick, when not e-mailing, are resting comfortably. Click here for Flickr album (154 photos)."

"Doug?" Lola asked without turning around.

"Mmm?"

"If—*when*—I'm pregnant, we cannot give the baby a working title. Not even if we think it's something we'll never, ever use in a million years, like Beowulf, or Ashlee. Okay?"

"Okay. What? Why?"

"I'm forwarding you something."

"Not even Kal-El?" came Doug's voice.

"No way."

Lola then saw that her long-suffering friend Sylvie had responded, only to Lola, to Oona's e-mail.

"Lo, listen, it's way too early to get excited, but, well, I'm excited and I wanted to tell you: I'm a teeny bit pregnant," she wrote. "So far it's just a double pink line in its mother's eyes, so all sorts of horrible stuff could still happen, etc., etc., but right now, I'm happy just to be nominated. Thanks for talking the other day. I'll keep you posted. XO, Sylvie. P.S. For the moment, we're calling it Kevin Federline."

"Hey, Sylvie is pregnant," Lola told Doug, still facing her computer.

"That's great!" said Doug, still facing his. "Anything else you want to tell me? I know it's only been like twenty minutes since we, you know, but hey, we live in a high-speed age."

"No no," Lola blushed, "just an e-mail baby boom."

"All rooty, just keep me in the loop," Doug called from his side.

"Roger," said Lola.

"I prefer Rogue," said Doug. "If we're still talking names."

"Fine, but Rogue's a girl," said Lola, smiling to herself.

"God, I lov—"

"A mutant, right? Absorbs other people's superpowers through contact with their skin?"

"Seriously. Please have my baby," said Doug.

Lola paused. "I'm getting there," she said. She wheeled halfway round in her chair, kissed Doug's head, and then completed the circle back to her keyboard.

Just a bit of research before I start that book proposal.
Lola clicked over to *Royalty*.

Chick Lit Killer Happy Ending: Girl Gets Guy
Posted by Page Proof

Lola whooped and pointed to the screen. Doug rolled over to
have a look.

After a dramatic confrontation on a bridge over Brooklyn's
Lundy Canal, police apprehended high-end interior landscape
designer Leo Guinness, 34, who has confessed to the series of
chick lit killings that have riveted the city and, at least tem-
porarily, boosted book sales. Only through her own derring-
do—and that of her adoring husband and best friend—did
writer Lola Somerville, 32, who had been duped by the alleged
killer into accepting a ride home, avoid the same fate, even
though recent sales of her critically acclaimed *Pink Slip* had
made her, technically, deserving of the killer's wrath.

One tear, then another crept into Lola's eyes. One for the joy
of vindication, one for the sadness of how it had come to pass.

Mr. Guinness, apparently, had been acting out of deranged love
for—

The phone rang.
Gotta be my mom or Annabel. Lola grabbed the receiver with-
out checking the caller ID. "Hi."
"Lola?"
Uh-oh.
"Yes, sorry. This is Lola. Who's calling, please?"
"Lola! Dixie Desmond here."
Well! It had been a dog's age since Lola had heard her agent's

voice. Clearly she was calling to tell Lola she had to get going, this morning, on her book about the murders.

"Saw your name on *Royalty* this morning—brava! Reminded me that I hadn't called to offer kudos on making the bestseller list," said Dixie.

Dixie was old-school, which Lola loved. Turned her nose up at e-mail, still called her secretary her secretary. She wore reading glasses on a chain around her neck. She was a person of middle age who actually ate lunch at lunch meetings; in other words, normal. Considering Dixie had probably never even held an iPod, it was a wonder she was able to nose out current trends.

"Thanks, Dixie," said Lola. And now, here comes the book idea.

"And, of course, I'm just glad you're okay, what with last night's kerfuffle and all."

"Thanks," said Lola. "Me, too."

Okay, pleasantries out of the way. Any second now.

"Anything else to report?" asked Dixie. "Not that your life hasn't been a thrill a minute lately."

"Uh—" Lola began. "Well, actually, it *has* been exciting. I'd actually been involved in the murders, I mean, not in a bad way, since the beginning."

"Oh, I know," said Dixie. "Very impressive."

"So I was thinking," said Lola. Looks like, once again, I'm going to have to do this my own damn self. "How about a book about that? You know, *The Inside Story of the Chick Lit Killings*, kind of thing. Sort of . . . an investigative memoir. Sebastian Junger meets V. I. Warshawski meets . . . Plum Sykes."

"It's a terrific idea, Lola," said Dixie.

Oh, yay! Lola's arms shot up in victory. At this point, Doug had turned to watch.

"So terrific, in fact, that it's been done," said Dixie. "I'm afraid your friend Wally Seaport sold that very book this morning."

Fifty-four

Lola clonked her forehead down on her keyboard, making her browser twitter in irritation and causing her *Ciao, Italiano!* CD-ROM, unused for months, to start asking directions to the Ponte Vecchio. Doug rolled his chair over, flipped Lola's hair over to the right side of her head, and hit a few buttons to shut Fabrizio up.

God*damn* it, thought Lola, still flopped forward.

God. Damn. It.

I mean, yes, I am so glad—*seriously* glad—that I helped catch the killer, to the degree that I did, before he hurt anyone else. I'm happy in principle to, you know, fight evil.

But will no one, *no one* give me a freaking break?

". . . as soon as you have a moment," Dixie Desmond had continued.

Lola flung her head back up. "I'm sorry, Dixie, my phone did something weird. What were you just saying?" She scribbled "Wally got the deal" on a corner of paper and passed it to Doug. He shook his head and grabbed her hand.

"Oh, just that I really would like to see a new proposal from you, Lola. Your voice is so authentic, attention's back on you and *Pink Slip*—the iron is hot," said Dixie. "Let's strike."

This, at least, was good to hear.

"Just no chick lit," said Dixie.

"Why, you think it's played out?" asked Lola.

"Oh, hardly," said Dixie. "But I just lured that lovely Blanca Palette away from her old agency, and I've just also signed someone else with a truly fresh, gritty voice. Name's Destiny. Runs a car service. A real hot ticket. So, I'm afraid, my own women's commercial fiction plate is full."

"I understand," said Lola.

Gah.

"Oh! And! Small world. Looks like I'll also be working with your detective friend and his wife. The Bobbseys. Soon as they're back from leave. A memoir about New York's finest overcoming infertility. Working title: *The Thin Pink Line*."

"Sounds great," Lola said.

"Right-o," said Dixie. "No one wants to read those fertility-guilt books anymore. That *Rotten Eggs* book, don't know if you've heard of it—apparently they keep scaling down the first print run. It'll be dead in the water."

Lola took a moment from her umbrage to give Sylvie a mental high five. "Okay, Dixie, I'll definitely put on my thinking cap." *Again*, she added sourly to herself.

"Capital," said Dixie. "By the way, how's that marvelous husband of yours?"

"Marvelous," smiled Lola, turning just far enough to kick Doug's foot.

"Good. I still remember him from your book party," said Dixie. "You two have such a nice rapport. Very Stiller and Meara."

Lola laughed. "Though I think I'm the Stiller."

"Probably so," said Dixie. "Anyway, I'm looking forward to your next brilliant idea."

"So am I," said Lola.

Just as she hung up with Dixie, the phone rang again. Detective Bobbsey.

"Detective! Congratulations!"

"Thank you, Ms. Somerville. Everyone's doing fine. We got ourselves a great little Bradley, Jr., here," he said. "Sleeping now, but soon's he wakes up we'll be prepping him for the Academy."

"That's just great, Detective. I'm so happy for you both. And you get to write about your . . . fertility . . . journey! I just heard."

"Yes, ma'am. So thank you for that. And for nabbing the killer while we were busy creating life," he said. "Deep."

"Well, you're welcome. But why thank me for the book?"

"You're an inspiration. So were your late friends. Your book is terrific."

"Let me guess. Beach bag?"

"Nope. Bought it myself. Wife tracked down your agent, you know the rest. Hope you don't mind."

"Hardly. I'm so glad it all worked out."

"Oops, looks like we've got company—Junior's uncle," said Bobbsey. "Which reminds me: heard you met my twin brother."

"Your twin brother," Lola repeated, foggy. "I thought you said you didn't have a twin brother."

"Nope, I just said my twin wasn't my partner. But my bro is also a detective, also a fan of the chick lit. And also very, very nearsighted."

No way. "Reading Guy? Reading Guy is your twin brother?"

Doug spun back around in his chair.

"Yeah, Bailey said that's what you call him. Fraternal," said Bobbsey. "And here right now, bearing a large, misshapen gift that I fear will produce unwelcome noises." His voice dropped to a whisper. "Why can't people just buy from the registry?"

"Well," said Lola. "Give Read—er, Bailey, my best."

"Will do. And Ms. Somerville, may we call you if we hit any, what do they call it, writers' blocks?"

"Of course, Detective," Lola said. "Of course."

Her other line beeped as she said good-bye.

Quentin. Who was, no doubt, going to be the one who'd really help the detectives with their writers' blocks.

"Lola, listen, I heard the whole deal, obviously, with Leo and all, and I just wanted to thank you again for everything," he said. "You know, I never really liked that Euro-bozo in the first place," he said.

"You are very, very welcome," said Lola, fiddling with a pen. "Actually, Leo's from Oxnard."

"I know, but you know."

"I know," said Lola.

"Also, I decided I'm getting out of the business. The writing business. The crossword writing business," said Quentin.

"Really?" said Lola.

"Yeah. It's . . . a dirty job. Hard to believe, I know. But I just quit this morning."

"Wow, Quentin, this is a big deal," said Lola. "So what next?"

"Small and exotic animals."

"I'm sorry, what?"

"Terrible what happened to that illegal kinkajou. She only bit out of fear, you know!" said Quentin. "First I'm starting an internship at the zoo—the toxicologist who saved Penny, who by the way I think I might be dating if I decide I'm ready, her brother works there, and he set me up. Meanwhile, I'm applying to veterinary school."

"You're kidding."

"I realize it's a bit of an about-face," Quentin admitted. "But it's something I have to do. And given that it's not 'artistic,' my cardiologist mother will subsidize. Not people-doctoring, of course, but close enough."

"Right, she always wanted you to go to medical school?"

"That, and at this point she's seen how dangerous literature is," said Quentin. "Oops, hang on." Lola heard some banging around in the background. "I'm just on my way out to clear my head with a bike ride."

A thought that had been leaning on the outer edge of Lola's consciousness suddenly broke through. She gripped the pen hard.

"Quentin, you're in your foyer?"

"Yeah."

"Is your doorman there?"

"Uh, yeah, sure. Why?"

"Can I speak to him for a second? I—I just wanted to thank him again for letting me in that night."

"Sure, I guess—hang on."

"Moe?" Lola heard Quentin say, extra-loud and clear. "My friend, my friend Lola Somerville, she came by the other night? She wants to talk to you for a sec."

There was a pause and some shuffling.

"Hello, young lady."

"Hi there, uh, Moe. I won't take too much of your time. Can I just ask you a few quick questions?"

"Nice gal like you? Moe's got all day."

"Thanks. You can just answer yes or no, if—if you prefer. That is, if you know what I mean."

"Aye, aye."

If I'm wrong, he'll think I'm a complete loon. Probably already does. But at this point, what have I got to lose?

Lola plunged forward with her hunch. "Remember that envelope you gave me that night?"

"Yes'm."

"Did you give it to me on purpose?"

"Yes'm."

"Because you wanted me to know what was inside?"

"Yes'm."

Lola snapped her fingers. Bingo.

"So . . . why?"

Oops. Not yes or no. But this was the money question.

And Moe, discreet doorman to the core, was right there with the answer.

"Loved *Pink Slip*," he replied. "Read it in one shift. Know the whole backstory, so on, so forth."

"You did? You do? Thanks!" Lola gushed, forgetting her mission for a moment.

"Yes'm. Terrible what's going on these days."

Lola paused. Does he mean what I think he means? Could my wild intuition actually have been a hundred percent right?

"You mean . . . you know what kind of work Quentin does, who he works for—"

"I'm a doorman," Moe said with some pride. Meaning: *I know everything.*

"And . . . you don't like it."

"No, ma'am."

Turns out I am a genius after all, thought Lola. "So. Right. You recognized me, had the envelope, took the opportunity to give it to me, but not in a way that would ever look suspicious on the security camera, on the off chance that I'd somehow be inspired to snoop and start asking questions, maybe figure out what this Cover outfit really is," she pronounced.

"I knew you were a smart young lady."

"Well, Moe, you've been very helpful," she said.

"I know," he said.

Quentin got back on the phone. "Guess he's a fan," he said. "When you were in the news, and then when your book came out, I kinda showed off that I know you."

"Dork," Lola teased.

"Anyway, honestly, I owe you."

Lola tapped the pen on her desk six, seven, eight times. "What's an eight-letter word f—"

"Indebted," said Quentin. "Beholden."

"Damn, you're good," said Lola. "But just kidding. You're really not. Indebted, I mean."

"Okay, then. Grateful. Thankful."

Lola smiled. "Quentin, have a great ride."

"Doug, can you take a quick break? Come for a little walk with me?" asked Lola.

"Gimme five minutes?" he asked. "Just finishing this Wikipedia entry on CMYK/RGB conversions."

"Oh, why don't you let me do that?" Lola teased.

She put on a little sunscreen, brushed out her hair, pulled some dead leaves off a ficus, walked around the living room, ate some strawberries, glanced at the *New York Times* lying untouched on the kitchen table. According to the Styles section, which had recently gone daily, knitting was hot, the eighties were back, and more and more women were smoking cigars. What, Lola thought, did they just deliver the paper from 2001?

"Where to?" Doug came in and glanced inside the fridge. "We need half and half."

"Can we stop at the book idea store?"

"Sure," said Doug. "We're out?"

Lola smiled ruefully.

They left the house, turning away from the bridge over the canal. Even before noon, the sun was burning high and hot. Doug steered them to the shady side of the street.

"Hang on." Lola doubled back to the mailbox on the corner. The pickup time label on the inside of the chute handle was covered with looping black graffiti. She took Quentin's check from The Cover out of her bag and dropped it into the box. Inside an envelope wiped clean of fingerprints and addressed, with her left hand, to Wally Seaport.

Surely they would reissue Quentin's check—perhaps his last.

And meanwhile, she'd let Wally investigate The Cover, maybe connect a few dots, write the exposé that's been waiting to happen.

Lola felt a bit bad about her potential role in revealing that authors like Mimi, Daphne, and Honey had had so much "help." But if The Cover's reach was as far as it seemed, their involvement was but a drop in the bucket. And as for their current contracts, there was no reason Annabel wouldn't keep her deal with her publisher; Quentin, whose actions were not so much wrong as annoying, would likely come out clean.

"Mailing anything interesting?" Doug asked. He then frowned in mock horror. "You don't pay bills with actual checks, do you?"

"Actually, in this case, yes," said Lola. *He will be so proud of me for handing this one off.* "See, the part I hadn't had a chance to tell you yet—"

Her phone rang.

Doug clapped his hands. "Your phone! Your favorite!"

Lola punched him in the arm.

"Hello?"

"Lola, so sorry to bother you on your cellular, but I just had an inspiration."

"No problem at all, Dixie." Lola stopped walking and raised her eyebrows at Doug. This was interesting. Dixie hated cell phones. She refused to use them except for matters of colossal importance.

"I was thinking about you and your husband. Your collaboration in the Leo Guinness affair. How well you seem to work together. How well do you think you would *work* together?"

"Like, *work* work? Probably pretty well, actually," said Lola.

"And pretty fast?"

"When can we start?" asked Lola.

"Start what?" Doug mouthed.

"Good girl. Here's the inspiration. A marriage guide. A *hip* marriage guide. Not that self-help pabulum that no one like you would be caught dead with on your nightstand. A guide for people like you. There are hip dating guides, there are hip parenting guides, but nothing for preeps like you."

"Preeps?"

"Pre-parents. It's a whole psychographic. Never mind. Are you with me?"

Dixie was practically breathless. This was the most excited Lola had ever heard her sound.

And this was the most excited Lola had felt in a long time. Her earlier reservations about branding herself professionally as one-half of a husband-and-wife team had dissolved, and not just because an agent was finally freaking calling her with an idea.

I am so tired of trying so hard to prove myself, Lola thought, *to friends, to editors, to the goddamn* New York Day *books section. Who on earth would think less of me if I let someone, someone who happens to be my beloved full partner in everything except possibly scented candles, share the driving? I am officially ready to stop with the clenched-hands, gritted-teeth efforts to control everything and instead take on what the universe seems to be offering me, even a universe that requires a fifteen percent commission.*

"Well, I guess I wouldn't be a good husband-wife team player if I didn't discuss this proposition with my husband first, would I?"

"Oh please, go ahead. But get back to me fast. This is a hot one," said Dixie. "And Lola?"

"Mmmhmm?" Lola was practically hopping on one foot at this point. Doug was smiling back at her, still having no idea why.

"Just don't use the term *team player* in the proposal."

"She wants us to write what?" asked Doug.

"We can totally do it," said Lola. "Between my experience, your 'fresh new voice'-ness, and the weirdness about communication and trust we just went through, we're all over it. The rest, we research." She was on a roll. "You can fit it in after work and stuff, can't you?"

Doug pondered for a second, but he was nodding already.

"Sure, monkey, yeah. *Yeah,*" he said. "I actually think we can do it. It'll probably be fun, huh? Plus, we're basically talking about getting paid to spend time together, so."

Lola flung her arms around his neck, kicking one leg back and up for old-fashioned emphasis.

Her cell phone beeped.

"See? Not my favorite," she said, not budging.

"You should get it," said Doug. "Could be Scorsese."

"All right," Lola said, disengaging herself. It was a text message. From Wilma Vouch.

Yr mom gave me yr #. Thank u so much 4 yr help w/everything. Let me take u 2 to lunch @ Bergdorf's sometime. Not that the cops believed me, but I go there all the time 4 the lobster club. Also, great bathrooms.

Beep. Another text message.

11:17 AM, antisocialclimber, hot sh*t writer Lola Somerville, running errands in NoWay, adorable as always

"Oh my God." Lola thrust the phone toward Doug. Before he could react, it rang.

"I'm so sorry, that was just me," Annabel admitted, laughing.

Lola joined her, cracking up. "You suck-slash-rule!"

"Couldn't resist. Checked with Doug, he said you were running out to do a couple things, so . . ." said Annabel. "Point is, I know it's, like, trivial, but you totally deserve someone to post that to Celebuphone. I know *I* don't count, but . . ."

"Actually, Bella?" said Lola. "You do."

Outside their favorite doorknob store, Lola stopped Doug and looked him in the eye. "And sweetie? I'm all about the breeding. Just . . . soon. Very soon. Really," she said. "I was getting there even before the book idea thing. I just need . . . a few more good nights of sleep. Then we can start having some not so good nights of sleep." She kissed his cheek. "Right now, just for today, let's say the book can be our baby."

"Deal," Doug said with a grin, kissing her right back. "Long as I get to pick the name."